PROJECT
MULBERRY

PROJECT MULBERRY

Linda Sue Park

HOUGHTON MIFFLIN HARCOURT
BOSTON NEW YORK

For information about permission to reproduce selections from this book,
write to trade.permissions@hmhco.com or to Permissions,
Houghton Mifflin Harcourt Publishing Company,
3 Park Avenue, 19th Floor, New York, New York 10016.

www.hmhco.com
The text of this book is set in 13-point Goudy.

The Library of Congress has cataloged the hardcover edition as follows:

Library of Congress Cataloging-in-Publication Data
Park, Linda Sue.
Project mulberry / by Linda Sue Park.
p. cm.
Summary: While working on a project for an after-school club, Julia, a
Korean American girl, and her friend Patrick learn not just about silk-
worms, but also about tolerance, prejudice, friendship, patience, and more.
Between the chapters are short dialogues between the author and main
character about the writing of the book.
1. Korean Americans—Juvenile fiction. [1. Korean Americans—Fiction.
2. Silkworms—Fiction. 3. Prejudices—Fiction. 4. Friendship—Fiction.
5. Family life—Illinois—Fiction. 6. Illinois—Fiction. 7. Authorship—
Fiction.] I. Title.
PZ7.P2213Pr 2005
[Fic]—dc22
2004018159

ISBN: 978-0-618-47786-9 hardcover
ISBN: 978-0-544-93521-1 paperback
Printed in the United States of America
DOC 10 9 8 7 6
4500752888

To Julie, Julie, Julia, and Julia

PROJECT MULBERRY

ONE

PATRICK AND I became friends because of a vegetable.

Not just any vegetable.

A cabbage.

And not just any old cabbage. A Korean pickled cabbage. Which isn't a round cabbage like Peter Rabbit would eat, but a longer, leafier kind. It gets cut up and salted and packed in big jars with lots of garlic, green onions, and hot red pepper, and then it's called *kimchee*. Kimchee is really spicy. Koreans eat it for breakfast, lunch, and dinner.

I don't like kimchee. My mom says that when I was little, I used to eat it. She'd rinse off the spiciness and give me a bite or two. When I got to be six or seven years old, she stopped rinsing it. Most Korean mothers do that, and most Korean kids keep eating it.

Not me. I hated the spiciness, and I still do. My mom keeps telling me I should eat it because it's refreshing. But what's so refreshing about having your mouth on fire?

My family used to tease me about not liking kimchee. My dad said maybe it meant I wasn't really Korean. "We should have your DNA tested," he'd tell me. The seven-year-old snotbrain named Kenny who lives with us — otherwise known as my little brother — would wave big pieces in front of me and threaten to force me to eat them.

Another thing about kimchee is, it has a really strong smell. Even though it's stored in jars, you can still smell it, right through the jar and the refrigerator door. It sends out these feelers through the whole house.

Three years ago, when I was in fourth grade, we were living in Chicago. I'd made friends with a girl named Sarah. The first time she came over to play, she stopped dead in the entryway and said, "*Eww! What's that smell?*"

I'd never really noticed it. Smells are funny that way—they can sort of disappear if you live with them all the time. But Sarah was so grossed out that I was really embarrassed.

The exact same thing happened again a few weeks later, this time with two friends, a boy named Michael and his sister, Lily. They *both* stopped dead in their tracks and grabbed their noses. Then they insisted that we play outside because they couldn't stand the smell.

I asked my mom to stop making kimchee, but she told me I was being unreasonable.

When we moved to Plainfield two years ago, our new apartment didn't smell like kimchee—for about half a day. Then my mom unpacked some groceries, including a big jar of kimchee. *Sigh.*

I met Patrick on our second day in Plainfield, a Saturday morning. Actually, I saw him on the first day; he was hanging around on his front steps three doors down, watching the movers. Him and his three brothers as well. I noticed him right away, not because of the way he looked — brown hair in a normal boy-haircut, a few freckles, a gap between his front teeth that predicted braces in his future — but because he seemed to be the closest to my age. The other three boys were little, younger even than Kenny.

On the second day, I took a break from unpacking and went out to have a good look at the neighborhood. There they were again, the four boys, like they'd never moved off the steps. This time there was a girl with them, too, but she was a lot older.

Patrick came down the steps and said hello and told me his name. I said hi back and told him mine.

"Can I see inside your house?" he asked.

"Sure," I said.

As we started down the sidewalk, we were suddenly surrounded by his three brothers.

"Can we come, too?"

"Patrick, we wanna see."

"Patrick, what's her name?"

Patrick stopped walking. "Claire!" he yelled.

The girl on the steps looked up from picking at her nails. "Yeah?" she said.

"Make them stay with you," Patrick said. "I can't go barging in with all of them."

"I'm leaving soon. Michelle is picking me up to go to the mall."

"Well, that means I'll be looking after them then. So you take them for now."

Claire stood up. "YOU BEEN ICKY!" she yelled.

At least that was what it sounded like to me, but later I learned that their names were Hugh, Ben, and Nicholas, and that Hugh was a year older than Ben and Nicky, who were twins, and that they usually got called "Hugh-Ben-Nicky" all in one breath.

"Aw—"

"Patrick—"

"Pleeeeease can we—"

"Hugh, let's go see if there are any cookies," Claire said.

Hugh let go of Patrick's arm and turned back toward their house. Ben and Nicky trotted after him. Patrick grinned at me. "If you get Hugh to do something, you've got all three of them," he explained.

As we walked in the door of my house, Patrick tilted his head and sniffed.

I braced myself for his reaction.

"Whoa," he said. "What's that? It smells great!"

That was the beginning of Patrick's love affair with kimchee. Whenever he eats dinner with us, my mom puts one bowl of kimchee on the table for the family and gives Patrick a whole private bowl for himself. He eats it in huge mouthfuls, sometimes without even adding any rice. I can hardly stand to watch him.

Maybe he's the one who needs his DNA tested.

"Goats."

"No."

"Sheep."

"No."

"Swine."

"*Wine?*"

Patrick and I were sitting on the floor of my room. He was reading aloud from a pamphlet. I was sewing up one of the cushions I keep on my bed. It had split the week before when we had a pillow fight, and the stuffing was falling out.

Patrick snorted. "Not wine, *ssswine*. You think

they'd let us anywhere near alcohol? Anyway, we've already decided to do an animal project. Wine is not an animal."

Patrick and I had just joined the Wiggle Club. Its real name is the Work-Grow-Give-Live! Club (Plainfield Chapter), which means its initials are WGGL, which is why all the kids call it Wiggle.

The Wiggle Club is supposed to teach kids about farming. Or at least it started out like that, a long time ago. It used to be for kids who lived on farms, far apart from each other, and it gave them a way to get together. These days, hardly anyone lives on farms; most of the land has been taken over by giant companies. Then the Wiggle clubs got started in cities and suburbs, so now we have one in Plainfield.

That's what Mr. Maxwell told us, anyway. He's the guy who runs the Wiggle Club, and he owns one of the only small farms left near Plainfield.

In January, club members sign up to do a project. They work on it for months, and the best ones get chosen to be exhibited at the state fair in August. Now it was March, and everyone else in the club had been working on their projects for a couple of months. Patrick and I had signed up only a week ago, so we were going to have to work fast.

We'd just attended our first meeting, where we decided we'd do an Animal Husbandry project.

"Mr. Maxwell?" Patrick had waved his hand. "Why is it called Animal *Husbandry*? Are we only allowed to work with male animals?"

Mr. Maxwell laughed. "No, Patrick, we work with both male and female animals. It's called *husbandry* because it's raising animals, taking care of them—"

Patrick interrupted him. "Then why isn't it called Animal *Wifery*? Wives take care of stuff—I mean, like raising babies—more than husbands do, don't they?"

Patrick isn't a rude person, but he really gets into things sometimes, and his ideas sort of pop out of him like he doesn't have any control over them.

His question made Mr. Maxwell pause a second. "Hmm. I think maybe it's because the word 'husband' has another meaning, one that not many people use anymore. It means to guard or watch over—like if someone's resting, we say they're 'husbanding their strength.'"

Patrick thought it over. He said, "Okay, I get

it. But wouldn't it be fairer just to call it Animal *Parentry?*"

That made Mr. Maxwell laugh again. "That *would* be fairer. Maybe you could start a campaign to change it. In the meantime—" He handed Patrick a Wiggle pamphlet on Animal Husbandry projects.

Patrick began reading it right away. He *loves* to read. He goes to the library all the time, and if he reads something interesting, he absolutely *has* to tell me about it. Once, when he was reading late at night about crows, he got so excited about how smart they are—they can learn to imitate sounds like car engines or dogs barking, he told me afterward—that he forgot how late it was and called me. My dad answered the phone and yelled at him. So now when Patrick's excited like that, he sends me an e-mail instead.

Wiggle meetings are held in the community recreation building a few blocks away from where I live. When the meeting ended, we walked to my house. We went up to my room, and that was when Patrick started reading the pamphlet out loud to me.

Patrick and I went through the whole list of animals.

It was discouraging. Most of them were big farm animals, and the rest were ordinary pets—dogs, cats, hamsters. We couldn't pick dogs or cats because the townhouses we live in don't allow pets that aren't in cages.

"We could do a hamster project," Patrick said doubtfully.

"Bo-o-o-ring," I said. I needed one more piece of thread to finish sewing up the cushion's seam. I licked the end of the thread, held up the needle, and took a deep breath. I always want to thread a needle on my first try—it's a thing with me. I poked the thread at the needle's eye.

Bingo.

"Reptiles," Patrick said. "Reptiles are more interesting. Maybe we could raise some kind of . . . of snake. No, not snakes—lizards. Lizards would be cool."

I pulled the thread halfway through and knotted the ends together. "I don't think so," I said as I started stitching. "My mom hates snakes, which means she probably wouldn't be too keen on lizards, either. And a snake at your house?" I snorted and shook my head.

Patrick nodded. "Gak," he said, which is what he always says when he's frustrated. "Yeah, you're right." Both of his parents work, so during the day his grandmother looks after the family. Patrick is the third oldest, after Claire and Katie, and then Hugh-Ben-Nicky. Their gram does the best she can, but nothing, and I mean *nothing,* is safe from those three.

Patrick shares a bedroom with his three brothers, and ages ago he started storing all his important stuff at my house. My mom doesn't mind, because he's very tidy about it. He even leaves his backpack here most days, and picks it up every morning when we walk to school. It's easy, because we always do our homework together anyway.

"Maybe we should do a gardening project instead," Patrick said. "Remember that girl Mr. Maxwell told us about who grew three different kinds of strawberries, and made jam from them, and wrote about which made the best jam—"

"Bo-o-o-ring," I said again.

"Well, don't forget, Jules, she won a prize at the state fair."

Patrick usually calls me Jules, which I kind of like.

Everyone else calls me Julia. A long time ago I tried out "Pat" in my head as a nickname for him, but it didn't seem to fit.

"Yeah, but not for the gardening," I said. "She won a ribbon for the *jam.* For the cooking part—you know, that cooking and sewing category."

"Domestic Arts," Patrick said. "But it was still a really good project. Mr. Maxwell said so, because it counted in two categories, Gardening and Domestic Arts. I wish we could think of an animal project like that."

Patrick looked at the alarm clock on the bedside table. It was almost five o'clock. "I'd better go," he said. Now that his older sisters are in high school, they're almost never home, and Patrick usually helps his gram give Hugh-Ben-Nicky an early supper. He stood up and put the pamphlet next to the clock. "I'm leaving this here. Read it before you go to bed. I've already read it, so I'll think about it. Maybe one of us will wake up with a good idea."

That's one of Patrick's favorite theories. He read somewhere that people remember stuff better if they read or think about it right before they fall asleep. We always try to study for a test together at bedtime, on the phone or by instant messaging.

I glanced at the pamphlet as we left the room. It would probably take a while before I got around to reading it. I don't like to read, not the way Patrick does.

Besides, he reads enough for both of us.

I've got another story to tell you, and I'm going to do it here, between the chapters.

Every story has another story inside, but you don't usually get to read the inside one. It's deleted or torn up or maybe filed away before the story becomes a book; lots of times it doesn't even get written down in the first place. If you'd rather read my story without interruption, you can skip these sections. Really and truly. I hereby give you official permission.

But if you're interested in learning about how this book was written—background informa-tion, mistakes, maybe even a secret or two

—you've come to the right place. Some people like that sort of thing. It's mostly conversations between me and the author, Ms. Park. We had a lot of discussions while she was writing. Here we go.

Me: *Why am I named Julia?*

Ms. Park: *You're named after my sister. Sort of. Her name is Julie.*

Me: *What about Patrick?*

Ms. Park: *Oh, that's just a name I like. But his character is partly based on a boy named Mark who lived across the street from me when I was growing up. Mark had five or six brothers and sisters, and he always had some kind of project going. I liked hanging out with him and was sad when he moved away after only a year in the neighborhood. I guess writing about Patrick is a way for me to spend more time with Mark.*

Me: *Do you know what's going to happen in the story? Do you already know the ending?*

Ms. Park: *I have a general idea of how I want the story to go, but nothing definite yet. Really just you and Patrick and the Wiggle project—that's all I've got so far.*

Me: *Hmm. It looks like you could use some help. Good thing I'm here. And I have one more question. That part about the friends who thought the house smelled awful. Did that really happen?*

Ms. Park: *To me or to you?*

Me: *To you, of course. I know it happened to me.*

Ms. Park: *Yes. But it happened to me in third grade, not fourth grade.*

Me: *Is that, like, legal? To change stuff like that?*

Ms. Park: *It is if you're writing fiction. . . .*

Fiction is about the truth, even if it's not always factual. I changed the fact about the grade, but not the truth about the feelings. Get it?

Me: *Yeah. I think so.*

Okay, do you see how this is going to work? On to chapter 2 now, and I'll see you on the other side.

TWO

WAIT," I SAID, stopping in the doorway. "Come back."

Patrick was almost at the stairs. "What?" he said.

"Everything in your pockets, please," I said, holding out my hand. "Unless you've checked already?"

"Um, no," Patrick muttered. "Okay, here." He reached into his jeans pocket, took out the contents, and showed me: A quarter, two pennies, a paper clip, a ball of lint, and a rather furry-looking cough drop.

"Yuck," I said, pointing to the cough drop. "Is that the same one from last time?"

He grinned. "Probably."

I took the quarter from him. We looked at it together.

Patrick and I were collecting and studying the state quarters. We'd bought special folders that had a slot for each one. Patrick kept track of which ones we needed, and looked up information about the little images on the backs of the quarters—the horse for Kentucky, the tree for Connecticut. He also had a little notebook to record when and where we found each one.

I was in charge of finding the quarters. That was pretty much the way we always worked. Patrick did the reading part, the research. I did the hands-on stuff—whatever needed to be cut and pasted or built or painted or sewn. Of course, we weren't very strict about it. Sometimes I'd do some of the reading, and Patrick would help with the making part. But we had our main jobs, and it suited us both.

Like with the quarters. To me, the exciting part was looking for them; whenever I got a quarter, I checked it out right away. That part drove Patrick

crazy. He almost always forgot to look at his quarters—I had to remind him most of the time—and
if he remembered, they usually weren't the ones we
needed. He'd get mad at himself for forgetting, or
mad at the quarters if they weren't the right ones. But
he loved looking up the stories about the pictures on
the coins.

Connecticut was my favorite quarter. It was
Patrick's favorite, too. I liked it because the tree was
so pretty; I wondered how hard it had been for someone to carve all those tiny branches. And maybe I
also liked it because it was on my mind a lot: I was
having no luck finding a second Connecticut. I had
two quarters from lots of other states, but still only
one Connecticut.

Patrick liked Connecticut because of the story
about the tree. It was sort of a spy story. Way back
in colonial times, the king of England tried to take
away Connecticut's government charter. There was
this meeting where the king's men were going to tear
up the charter, and suddenly the candles got blown
out so the room was all dark, and when they got the
candles lit again, the charter was gone. Some guy had

escaped with it, and hid it in a hollow oak tree—the tree on the coin. It even has "The Charter Oak" in teeny letters.

We never put the quarters into the folders until I'd found two of the same state, so both of our Connecticut slots were still empty.

I turned over Patrick's quarter.

"New York," I said.

"Dang it."

We already had our New Yorks.

"Bye, Patrick," my mom said. She must have heard us coming down the stairs, because she was all ready for him. Her chopsticks were loaded with a bite of rice and a few pieces of kimchee. Patrick opened wide, and she popped that mouthful right in.

"Thanks, Mrs. Song," he said, not very clearly because he was chewing. "Bye, Julia."

This is their routine whenever Patrick leaves our house at dinnertime. We have rice and kimchee for dinner almost every night, no matter what the main course is, and my mom always gives Patrick a bite as he goes out the door.

For dinner we were having beef short ribs—and rice and kimchee, of course. I love short ribs. I like picking them up in my hands and gnawing on them to get every last shred of meat.

"Patrick coming back after supper?" my mom asked.

"Yup," I said. "We haven't done our homework because of the meeting, and afterward we talked about our project."

My dad said, "What project?"

I picked up a rib. "Wiggle project," I said. "We want to do something with animals."

"A report on an animal?" My dad again.

"No, it's a hands-on thing," I explained. "You have to work with a real animal. So they suggest all these things like sheep and cows and pigs, or else you can do pets. We can't do *any* of those."

"So if you do a cow project, you have to milk it yourself—something like that?"

"No, you have to raise it. In the old days, kids used to get a lamb or a calf or something from a farmer, and they'd learn how to feed it and take care of it. That kind of thing."

"Mom, if Julia gets an animal, can I have one, too? Can I have a dog?" That was Kenny.

"No pets," my dad said. He turned to my mom. "Didn't your family raise animals?"

My dad grew up in Seoul, which is the capital of Korea, a really big city. But my mom's family lived outside the city, and in those days Seoul didn't have many suburbs. It was mostly countryside.

"Not really," my mom said. "It's not like my family were farmers."

I knew that. I heard about it all the time — my parents were always saying that I had to get good grades because both of my grandfathers had been teachers.

"But almost everyone kept poultry," she went on. "I know a little bit about chickens."

"Could we —"

She didn't even let me finish. "No," she said immediately. "Chickens are a mess. And they need lots of space to run around and scratch and build nests. Besides, I'm sure it would be against zoning laws or something to keep chickens here."

Our apartment is a townhouse — one of a whole

line of skinny houses all stuck together. It has a little square of grass on one side of the front walk, and a back stoop big enough for the barbecue grill. But that's all. No yard.

"*Bawk*," Kenny said. "*Bawk-bawk*." He bent his arms and flapped them like wings. "I'm a chicken, *bawk-bawk-bawk*."

I'd had lots of practice over the years ignoring Kenny's dorkiness, but this time I couldn't. His flapping wing hit my arm, and the rib in my hand went flying. It landed in the kimchee bowl.

"Kenny!" I yelled.

"It was an accident!" he yelled back. "I didn't mean to!"

"Both of you, hush," my mom said. She picked up the rib and put it back on my plate. No way I was going to eat it now—it was all covered in kimchee juice. I kicked Kenny under the table.

"Mom!" he yelled. "Julia kicked me!"

What a baby. A snotbrain *and* a baby.

"Okay, that's enough," my dad said. "Julia, clear the table, please."

Kenny and my mom left the kitchen. He'd play a

computer game and my mom would watch the news while my dad and I cleaned up.

It wasn't fair that Kenny never had to help. My parents said he'd have to when he was older. Well, I was clearing the table when I was his age. Still, I liked that it was just me and my dad. It never took us long to clean up because we had a routine. Me standing at the table, my dad at the sink: I'd grab a plate, scrape it into the garbage can, hand it to him; he'd rinse it and put it in the dishwasher. By the time he did that, I had another plate ready for him. He didn't even have to look up; he'd just stick out his hand, and I'd put the plate right into it. We were like a machine —a scraping, rinsing, loading machine.

We were almost done when Patrick knocked at the door and came in. He wasn't a member of the family, so he knocked, but he was *almost* a member of the family, so he came in without waiting for anyone to answer. He yelled hi as he went up to my room to get his backpack, then came down again.

"Can I help?" he asked.

"It's okay, Patrick, we're almost finished," my dad said.

Patrick sat at the table and opened his backpack. Just then my mom came into the room.

"I thought of a project you might be able to do," she said quietly.

"Really?" I said at the same time that Patrick said, "What is it?" I stopped scraping the plate I was holding.

My mom's eyes twinkled at me.

"Worms," she said.

I stared at her for a second. *"Worms?"* I said.

My mom nodded.

"We'd raise worms?" I said. "You mean, like, for fishermen to use as bait?"

Right away a whole bunch of thoughts started jostling around in my mind. I turned to Patrick. "Maybe we could have them in an aquarium, but filled with dirt instead of water, and that way you could see them through the glass."

Patrick looked doubtful. "Worms," he said slowly. "I don't know. . . ."

Then he started talking faster. "I read a book a while ago. There was this part where the people released bags and bags full of ladybugs on a farm because they were good for the plants. Or something like that. Somebody had to raise those ladybugs to get so many bagfuls, didn't they? Maybe we could raise ladybugs—"

My mom laughed and held up her hand. "Slow down, you two. I wasn't thinking of earthworms. Or ladybugs."

I said, "Well, what other kind of worms . . . Oh, like caterpillars, you mean? 'The Life Cycle of the Monarch Butterfly' or something?"

I didn't mean to sound impatient—I knew my mom was only trying to help. But raising caterpillars was more like a science-fair project, not a Wiggle project.

"Sort of. No, not exactly." My mom took the plate out of my hand and gave it to my dad. "I was thinking you could do a silkworm project."

I stared at her with my mouth half-open.

"My grandmother raised silkworms in Korea," my mom said. "I used to help her. It's really quite interesting, and it's not like butterflies. I mean, it is in some ways, but it's more than that. Because at the end you get an actual product—the silk."

"It's sort of like sheep," Patrick said. "Only instead of sheep and wool, it's caterpillars and silk. . . ."

I was pretty sure I'd already known that silk came from silkworms. But I'd never really thought about it before.

"Exactly," my mom said. "It would be on a small scale, of course—you wouldn't end up with enough silk to make fabric. But you might get enough for some thread."

"Thread?" Patrick opened his eyes wide. He took a deep breath, swallowed, and sort of shook himself. Then he stood up and started pacing around the kitchen. "Jules, we can raise the—the caterpillars, and get thread from them, and then you can *sew* something with the thread, and we can enter the project in two categories—Animal Husbandry and Domestic Arts!"

He looked at me, his face all business. "I'll get started on the Internet—oh, wait," he said, and frowned at his watch. "It's not even seven-thirty. I can't do it yet."

Patrick knew our family's evening routine. Kenny got the computer until eight o'clock, and I got it after that.

"Homework comes first anyway, you two," my mom said.

I went to get my backpack, wondering when Patrick would notice that I was not one bit excited about doing a silkworm project.

Me: *Is there other stuff in my story so far that comes from real life?*

Ms. Park: *Yes. A bunch of things.*

Me: *Like what?*

Ms. Park: *Well, let's see. I hated kimchee when I was little. I like it now, but I didn't when I was your age.*

Me: *Wow. You can remember that far back?*

Ms. Park: *Very funny. I don't remember*

everything, of course. But parts of my childhood are quite vivid to me, and I like going there in my mind. You probably will, too, when you're older.

Me: *Did your parents grow up in Korea?*

Ms. Park: *Yes. And my father always did the dishes.*

Me: *Did you have a bratty younger brother? Is that why you put Kenny in the story?*

Ms. Park: *I have a younger brother and a younger sister. But neither of them was very bratty. I got along with them pretty well when we were kids.*

Me: *A sister would be much better. I have a great idea—why don't you delete all the stuff about Kenny and give me a sweet younger sister instead? Her name could be . . . Jessie. I like that name. Julia and Jessie—isn't that nice? And she could be really cute, and she could worship me—*

Ms. Park: *But I like Kenny. He's funny.*

Me: *Funny to you, maybe! To me he's a big pain!*

Ms. Park: *Well, I'm the one writing the story, so I get to decide. Kenny stays.*

Me: *Gak!*

THREE

WORKSHEET. EXPONENTS. WE had to write out the problem again the long way, and then give the answer in two different forms.

$10^2 \times 10^6$

Answer 1:_____
Answer 2:_____

I filled in the blanks:

$(10 \times 10) \times (10 \times 10 \times 10 \times 10 \times 10 \times 10)$

Answer 1: $\underline{10^8}$
Answer 2: $\underline{100,000,000}$

Bo-o-o-ring.

Patrick said that whoever invented exponents must have been either really lazy or really impatient. They got sick of writing all those zeroes, so they invented a way to do it quicker.

We finished the worksheet, then quizzed each other on our social studies unit. We'd already done Ancient Civilizations of the New World: North America, and now we were doing Ancient Civilizations of the New World: South and Central America. Today's homework was on the Maya. We were supposed to learn the countries that were now located where they used to live: Belize, El Salvador, Guatemala, and parts of Mexico. Patrick made up an acronym to help us remember the countries: BEG-Mex.

It was almost eight o'clock. "Come on, that's enough studying," he said, getting up off the floor. "We can start researching silkworms."

I looked down at the page in front of me. "You go ahead," I said. "I need to study a little more."

Patrick stopped at the kitchen door and turned back. "Okay," he said, "what is it?"

I had other good friends at school and on my soccer team—Emily and Carly played defense with me, and we hung around off the field, too. But I spent more time with Patrick than anyone else. Sometimes the other guys teased him about having a girlfriend, but it didn't seem to bother him. It didn't bother me, either. If those guys couldn't tell the difference between a friend and a girlfriend—well, that made them too dense to be worth worrying about.

One thing about being best friends for so long: When one of us is mad, the other almost always knows it without asking. This is usually a good thing. If I'm mad at Patrick, he knows right away rather than being clueless about it and making me even madder.

But once in a while I want to be mad privately. This was one of those times.

"What is *what*?" I said.

"Come on, Jules," he said. "You're mad about something, I can tell."

"Never mind," I muttered.

"Gak," he said. "I hate when you're like this." He stood there a little longer, but I didn't say anything more. He shrugged and went downstairs.

I almost called after him to say that I wasn't mad at *him*. Well, maybe I was, a little—at how he was just assuming we'd do a silkworm project without even discussing it. But that wasn't the main reason I was upset. And I didn't want to talk about the main reason, because it was sort of complicated.

I thought of Wiggle as a club that was all about country life—farming, raising animals, cooking and sewing, stuff they used to do in the old days. Big red barns. Cornfields. Hay rides. That kind of thing.

Silkworms just didn't seem like a good Wiggle project to me. They didn't fit into the big-red-barn picture. They were too . . . too . . .

Too *Korean.*

In Chicago there had been lots of other Korean families, and I'd had Korean friends. But not in Plainfield. We were the only Korean family in town.

In fact, on one of my first days of school here a bunch of girls had yelled "Chinka-chinka-Chinaman" at me on the playground. It made me feel really bad inside—so bad that I hated thinking about it. And, of course, the more I tried not to think about it, the more I thought about it. I was glad when that memory started to fade, and it hardly ever came up anymore.

It might be starting to sound like being Korean was a Huge Issue for me, but that wasn't true. I mean, when I was doing my math homework or watching TV or whatever, I wasn't constantly thinking stuff like, I *wish I wasn't Korean.*

Whenever I *did* think about it, though, it was because something was upsetting me. I didn't want my house to smell like kimchee. I didn't want kids to yell "Chinka-chinka-Chinaman" at me. And I didn't want to do something weird and Asian for the Wiggle Club.

I wanted a nice, normal, All-American, red-white-and-blue kind of project.

Patrick and I have done lots of projects together. The leaf collection in fifth grade. "Get to Know Your

Community" the same year. In sixth grade, we built a model of a water molecule, a Pleistocene-era miniature landscape, and a Revolutionary War diorama. And of course we had our quarters project outside of school.

So it made sense that we'd work on a Wiggle project together. But now I didn't know what to do. I knew what Patrick was like when he was excited. It would take me forever to talk him out of a silkworm project, and I'd have to tell him why I didn't want to do it, and he'd probably think I was being stupid and get really mad at me.

But maybe . . .

Maybe I wouldn't have to talk him out of it. In all my life, I'd never heard of anyone raising silkworms except my grandmother, who did it about a million years ago in Korea. So maybe it would be really hard to raise silkworms here. Maybe we wouldn't even be able to get started.

I could just wait and see. And if we ran into an impossible snag, we'd have to give up the idea, and it wouldn't be because of me.

I felt a lot better after I figured this out. I got

up and went into the living room. It was seven fifty-seven on the computer clock. Patrick was sitting next to the computer watching Kenny play a game.

"Three more minutes," Kenny whined at me. "You can't have it yet—I've got three more minutes to beat the boss."

"Two and a half now," I said. "Better not mess up—you won't have time to try again." Of course, my saying that made him mess up immediately, and he lost his last life.

"Julia!" he yelled. "You made me die!" Kenny only had two volume levels: whine and yell.

Patrick once told me that I was too hard on Kenny. "He's a little kid, Jules. Sheesh, you fight with him a lot more than I do with my whole family put together."

I didn't say what I was thinking, which was three things. One: Patrick had so many brothers and sisters that the fighting was sort of spread out instead of concentrated between two people. Two: Patrick spent as much time as he could at *my* house, so he couldn't fight with them when he was here. And three: All of Patrick's brothers and sisters multiplied by ten—no, multiplied by 10^{10} — wouldn't be anywhere near as bratty as the Snotbrain.

When Kenny was born, he was really cute. He'd sit in his baby chair and watch me all day long as I went around doing stuff, and whenever I stopped to talk to him, he'd give me a huge smile.

But then (loud scary music here, like in the movies) . . . he learned to crawl.

Who knew that a little baby — one that couldn't even *walk* yet — could be such a maelstrom of destruction? A maelstrom — a word I learned from Patrick, who had picked it up somewhere in his reading — is a giant, violent whirlpool. It had seemed like a very unusual word at the time, but a few months after I first heard it, I saw it on a computer game. It was a weapon you could use to destroy enemies. It was also the perfect word to describe what Kenny could be like.

Kenny the Maelstrom knocked down whatever I built. He scribbled on the pictures I drew, or ripped them to pieces. He chewed on stuff I left lying around. He *threw up* on my very favorite stuffed panda. My mom washed it, but after it came out of the dryer, it was rough and lumpy, not soft like it used to be.

As soon as Kenny learned to talk, we started fighting. When I was eight and he was three, he made me really, really mad. I can't remember now what he did, but it was so awful that I yelled, *"You—you—"* and I tried to think of the worst thing I could call him. *"You* SNOTBRAIN!"

Ever since then, that's been my nickname for him. But I never called him that around my parents. They had a no-name-calling rule. In general, I thought it was a good rule.

Except when it came to the Snotbrain.

Me: *Do you want my opinion? I am not happy with the way things are going here. I hate the project idea, Kenny is driving me nuts, and I still haven't found another Connecticut.*

Ms. Park: *Actually, no—I don't want your opinion. In fact, I have to admit, this is weird for me. I've written other books, and only once has a* character ever talked to me. You talk to me all the time, and I'm finding that hard to get used to.

Me: *Like right now, while you're in the—ahem—bathroom. Well, I don't care whether you want my opinion or not—you're getting it. That was a terrible chapter.*

Ms. Park: *Would it help if I said I'm sorry you're having such a hard time?*

Me: *If you were really sorry, you'd go back and rewrite it.*

Ms. Park: *You're the main character. You have to have a problem or two. If you didn't, there wouldn't be any story.*

Me: *In that case, how's this: Patrick and I get, like, five ideas for the project, five good American ideas, and they're all so brilliant that we can't decide which one to choose. That would be a much better problem.*

Ms. Park: *That would be a different story. Not the one I want to tell.*

Me: *But it's my story. I should have a vote.*

Ms. Park: *Okay. In the next chapter, I promise Kenny won't bother you as much. Now will you leave me alone for a while?*

Me: *Fair enough. But what about the other stuff?*

Ms. Park: *One thing at a time, please.*

FOUR

PATRICK SAT DOWN in the computer chair and typed *silkworms* into the search-engine box. I flopped down on the old armchair nearby. Across the room my parents were reading. Kenny had stormed upstairs after losing his game and had not come back down again to pester us, thank goodness.

While Patrick clicked and read, I did some hard thinking. Ideas jostled around in my brain and I tried to get them organized.

We had only a couple of months to work on our Wiggle project. It might take a little while before my plan worked and we could drop the silkworm idea. I didn't think we'd have time for a whole new project after that, so I needed to get started on something else.

Patrick wanted the silkworms to make thread . . . and then I was supposed to sew something with the thread, so we'd be able to enter our project as both an animal project and a sewing project. . . .

A sewing project. I could plan a sewing project, and when the silkworm part didn't work out, I'd be ready to do it with regular thread.

But what should I sew? It would have to be something really cool to have a chance of winning a prize at the state fair.

I thought about it some more. Wiggle sewing projects were usually clothes. Mr. Maxwell had shown us pictures of projects kids had done in other years. One girl had made mother-daughter dresses (gag). Another had sewn a lot of bright red fleece vests. On the back of each vest she'd embroidered *Oak Hill School and Home.* That was a boarding school for disabled kids in our town. On the front was a person's name. The girl had made these vests for the kids at Oak Hill

—the ones who were her age. When they went out on field trips, they wore the vests, and that bright red color made it easy for their teachers to keep track of them. Another double project: Domestic Arts *and* Community Service.

Thinking about those vests made me realize that what I really like isn't sewing—I mean, not on the machine. I like doing stuff by hand. That's a separate category in Wiggle; it's called Needlework.

In my parents' bedroom there was a framed picture of some flowers. Not painted flowers—embroidered ones. My mom made it ages ago, when she lived in Korea. It was really good; she'd used millions of tiny stitches. Maybe I could make something like it. . . .

"Mom," I said, "could you teach me how to embroider?"

Patrick glanced over at me. I answered before he could ask. "Embroidery," I said. "I'm gonna get started practicing for when we get the thread from the worms."

I hoped my face didn't show how I was feeling,

which was a little guilty. It wasn't a lie, but it wasn't the whole truth, either.

He gave me a thumbs-up and went back to clicking the mouse. It seemed like he'd already forgotten I was mad about something, which was fine with me —now that I had a plan, I wasn't mad anymore.

My mom put down her book, looking pleased. "I was thinking a while back that you might want to learn," she said. "Is your homework finished?"

I nodded.

"Then we can start right now."

She went upstairs for a few minutes and came back down carrying her sewing basket and an old plastic shopping bag. From the bag she took a wooden hoop and some white fabric. It turned out that the hoop was really two hoops that fit together tightly, one right inside the other. She unlocked a little clasp, and the two hoops came apart.

I went and sat next to her on the couch. She showed me how to put a square of fabric between the two hoops, and how to pull the fabric so it was nice and tight and smooth.

She'd also brought the embroidered picture from her room. Now she took the frame and started undoing the catches at the back. "A long time ago—I don't know how long, hundreds of years, maybe—Korean women decided they wanted to make their embroidery work different somehow," she said, "to set it apart from Japanese and Chinese embroidery."

She held up the piece of fabric and then turned it around so I could see the back.

Wow.

The back side looked exactly the same as the front. There wasn't a single knot or loose thread anywhere.

"Patrick, look." I took the picture from my mom and held it up so he could see it. Then I flipped it over.

He looked at it for about half a second. "Pretty," he said, and turned back to the screen.

He didn't get it.

"How did you do that?" I asked my mom. Never mind about Patrick for now. I'd explain it to him later.

"I can teach you," she said, "but not right away. You have to get good at the basic stitches first."

"It's like sewing, right?"

"Yes and no. It *is* like sewing, but there are also some differences, and you have to be a lot more precise, which makes it harder. Let's see how you do."

She was right. To start with, I had to put two pieces of thread through the eye of the needle instead of just one. It took me five tries! I thought it would only be *twice* as hard as putting one piece through, but it was exponents again — about 2^3 times harder.

After I finally got the needle threaded, my mom taught me the simplest stitch. Running stitch. You put the needle in and out and in and out of the fabric, and you end up with what looks like a dotted line. Easy.

My mom looked at my stitches. "Not bad," she said. "But a little uneven. In embroidery it's important that all your stitches be exactly the same size." Then she did five stitches to show me what she meant.

They were beautiful. Perfect. So even.

"Not just the stitches," she said. "The spaces in between have to be the same size, too. Because —"

"Because that's what makes the back side look the same as the front!" I exclaimed.

My mom nodded and smiled.

I was proud of myself for figuring that out.

Then I got so involved in trying to make perfect running stitches that I almost forgot Patrick was still there.

"Jules," he said, turning the swivel chair around so he could look at me. "We've got a problem."

"Good news first," Patrick said. "There are a whole bunch of places that sell the eggs. We can order them over the Internet. They're around ten bucks for twenty-five eggs."

Hmm—so it *was* possible to get silkworm eggs here. Then what was the problem?

"But it's no good us even ordering them," Patrick went on, "unless we can find a mulberry tree."

My mom made a little surprised noise. "That's right," she said. "I'd forgotten about that. We had a mulberry tree in our backyard in Korea. It was one of my jobs to pick leaves for the worms to eat."

"There's something called artificial silkworm food," Patrick said. "But it's really expensive, because you have to buy a huge amount. For, like, hundreds of caterpillars. And besides, they grow much better if they eat mulberry leaves. They won't eat any other kind."

A mulberry tree? Wasn't it a bush? That nursery rhyme, *Here we go round the mulberry bush, the mulberry bush, the mulberry bush* . . .

Patrick said what I was thinking. "I've never even heard of a mulberry tree. A mulberry *bush*, in that song for babies. But not a tree. I bet there isn't a single mulberry tree in all of Plainfield."

My mom turned to my dad. "*Yobo*," she said.

That's not his name—his name is Jay. Jae-woo in Korean, but people call him Jay. My mom's Korean name is Jung-sook, but everyone calls her June. *Yobo* is a Korean word that means "honey" or "dear." My mom and dad almost always called each other "*Yobo*."

"*Yobo*, don't you know someone with a mulberry tree?" my mom asked.

My dad lowered the newspaper. "What's that?" he said.

"Mulberries," my mom said. "Didn't someone

bring a mulberry pie to one of your office parties a while ago? Remember, you told me about it because you said you hadn't seen mulberries since Korea."

"Oh. Yes." My dad blinked a couple of times. Obviously, he hadn't been listening to the conversation, so now he was clueless. "I did tell you about that, didn't I."

"Dad!" I said. "Those mulberries—do you know where they came from?"

Patrick and I both waited for my dad's answer, but I knew it was for different reasons: Patrick hoping the mulberry tree was somewhere nearby, me hoping it wasn't.

"Wisconsin," my dad said.

Yesss. Wisconsin was hours away!

"The lady who made the pie, her mother lives in Wisconsin," my dad continued. "The lady went up there for a visit and brought back frozen mulberries from her mom's tree and made a pie for us." He smiled. "*Great* pie."

Sheesh. He was so out of it.

"Well," Patrick said slowly, "that's good news in a way. I was afraid maybe they only grew in the tropics or the desert or somewhere like that. At least now we know they *can* grow here."

"That's right," my mom said. "You need to ask around. Somebody in town might have a mulberry tree."

"We could ask Mr. Maxwell," Patrick said, looking a little more hopeful. "Maybe he would know."

"We won't see him for another week," I pointed out. "Not until the next Wiggle meeting."

"Gak," Patrick said. "But wait—I have an idea. There's something else we can do in the meantime. Jules, come over here and help me."

Ms. Park: *There! A whole chapter where Kenny didn't bother you once.*

Me: *Well, of course. You're not one of those people who don't keep their promises, are you? I hate that. But I have to say, it was a pretty short chapter. I think that's sort of cheating—you didn't have to keep him away for very long.*

Ms. Park: *For heaven's sake, he lives with you,*

and it's not a very big apartment. You're bound to run into him in most chapters.

Me: *And another thing. You'd better give me plenty of time in the story to practice my embroidery.*

Ms. Park: *I refuse to promise that. It's your responsibility. You have to organize your schedule, get your homework and your chores done, and not dilly-dally around. You should have plenty of time to do embroidery if you plan your time efficiently.*

Me: *Sheesh. You sound like my mom. But as you keep telling me, you're the writer. If you write a dilly-dallying scene, what choice do I have? Like how you made me have a brother instead of a sister.*

Ms. Park: *It's not that simple. I'm not always in control.*

Me: *Ha! You mean I'm the boss now? I get to decide everything?*

Ms. Park: *No, that's not what I meant. Neither of us is the boss. The story is the boss.*

Me: *How can the story be the boss?*

Ms. Park: *It's kind of hard to explain. Sometimes the story takes over, and I end up writing things I didn't expect. I think you'll understand later.*

Me: *I hate it when grownups say that.*

FIVE

THE NEXT MORNING, Patrick and I left early for school. Patrick had the duct tape, and I carried the flyers.

MULBERRY TREE NEEDED
Do you have a mulberry tree in your yard?
We need some leaves.
Please call Julia at 555-2139.

We got my mom's permission to use my phone number, because if anyone called Patrick's house when he wasn't home and one of the little kids answered, he'd never get the message. That was a possibility with the Snotbrain, too. But at least there was only one of him, and my mom usually answered the phone anyway.

Last night, Patrick had typed in the information, then I'd designed the flyer, centering the text and using a nice font. If I had really wanted us to find a mulberry tree, I'd have thought the flyers were a great idea. So I was pretending to be all enthusiastic about them.

I told Patrick the flyers were genius, and I really *did* think it was smart of him, but inside I was almost positive they wouldn't work. I had solid evidence that a mulberry tree would be practically impossible to find around here. And not just because of what my dad had said about that tree being in Wisconsin. I had other proof.

When Patrick and I did our leaf project in fifth grade, we got more leaves than anyone else in the class. We went all around our neighborhood and to other parts of Plainfield, too. The assignment was to collect fifteen leaves, but we had twenty-seven, which gave us a ton of extra credit. Three kinds of maple (red, silver, Japanese); four kinds of oak (pin, white, red, bur); sycamore, locust, gum, willow, birch—I can't remember them all now, but there were a bunch of fruit trees. Apple, peach, pear, plum, and a friend of my mom's even had a quince tree.

No mulberry.

If there had been a mulberry tree nearby, Patrick and I would have found it. In the whole class, there was only one kind of leaf someone else got that we didn't have, and it wasn't really fair, because it was from a hibiscus tree that grew in a pot and was taken inside for the winter.

That's why I was pretty sure the flyers wouldn't help, so I did my best to make them look good. We printed them on fluorescent green paper, and I made the font really big so you could read it from far away.

We stopped at several places on the way to school. The gas station on the corner of our street. The convenience store across from our school. Three or four big utility poles on busy corners.

The lady who worked at the gas station was really nice. I'd never met her before. My parents went to that gas station, but they used pay-at-the-pump, so I always just stayed in the car.

When we first went in to talk to her, I thought she was a little scary. She had orange hair piled sky-high and hairsprayed rock-solid, and she also had the worst teeth I'd ever seen. They were this nasty olive-green color. But she let us put the flyer up in the window and said she'd be sure to point it out to people.

That was Wednesday morning. I was pretty jumpy that day after school—every time the phone rang I was afraid it would be somebody saying they had a mulberry tree.

But nobody called that day.

No calls the next day, either.

And none on Friday.

I was right. There weren't any mulberry trees in our neighborhood.

By Saturday afternoon, even Patrick was sick of hanging around waiting for our phone to ring, so we walked to the convenience store to get slushies. I got the 79-cent size, and gave the cashier a dollar bill plus four pennies so my change would be a quarter.

Illinois.

Gak. I already had two Illinoises and had gotten at least a dozen more.

Still no Connecticut.

No calls Saturday, Sunday, or Monday. On Tuesday we went to the Wiggle meeting. This was another hurdle. If Mr. Maxwell knew where there was a mulberry tree, I'd be in trouble; I'd have to start all over again, hoping for a different snag.

The Wiggle meeting started out with bad news—bad for me, that is. Patrick went right to Mr. Maxwell and told him we wanted to do silkworms for our project. And Mr. Maxwell said okay. In fact, he seemed to think it was a great idea. "A first for me," he said. "Never had anyone do a silkworm project before. It'll be unique. Good job, kids."

I cheered up—secretly, of course—a minute later, when Mr. Maxwell told us that he didn't know anyone with a mulberry tree. "I'll ask around," he said. "You never know."

Everyone talked about how their projects were going. Abby brought in a pie every week. She was planning to enter the pie competition and was perfecting her crust. She gave each of us a bite or two and then would ask a million questions about the crust. "Was it flakier last week?" she'd say, or, "It's still not flaky enough, is it?" I wanted to be helpful, but I was hopeless at trying to remember—they all tasted good to me.

Tony and Nathan had baby tomato plants they were growing from seed. Angela had baby potato plants she was growing from the eyes of a bunch of different kinds of potatoes.

Kevin was raising a goose. The goose's name was Gossage. "The baseball player," Kevin said. "My dad's favorite pitcher." Patrick explained it to me. A while back there had been a Chicago White Sox pitcher named Rich Gossage, whose nickname was "Goose." Sometimes Kevin brought Gossage to the meeting to show us the tricks he was learning. Gossage could already honk on command and untie Kevin's shoelaces.

Everyone else was way ahead of us.

Patrick looked a little discouraged on our walk home. I decided it would be a good time to put my plan into action.

"The flyers didn't work," I said, "and Mr. Maxwell doesn't know anyone with a mulberry tree." I shook my head and sighed. "It's not looking good, Patrick —maybe we should think of a backup plan, just in case."

He scowled. "I don't want a backup," he said. "You heard Mr. Maxwell. He thinks it's a great idea for a project. There's gotta be a mulberry tree somewhere in this dumb town."

I was about to tell him that we could start thinking of other ideas and still look for a mulberry tree at the same time when someone shouted "Hey!" from behind us.

We turned around. It was the gas station lady. She was waving at us from the doorway.

"Hey, kids!" she called again.

We stood in the tiny office while the lady went back behind the counter. "Mr. Dixon comes in here once a week," she said. "Monday morning at ten-thirty, like clockwork. He always buys the exact same things: ten bucks' worth of gas and a roll of wintergreen mints."

I tried not to fidget. Why was she telling us this?

"Well, when he came in yesterday, I showed him your sign, like I said I would," she went on. "And he kinda mumbles, 'Mulberries.'" She made her voice low and grumbly, so I got the idea that he must be an old man.

"So I ask him, 'You know anybody who's got a mulberry tree?' And he says, 'Young lady'—I know, that must seem funny to you, him calling me a young lady, but compared to him I *am* young"—she laughed, showing all those green teeth. "Anyway, he says, 'Young lady, time was, everybody around here knew I had the only mulberry tree in town.'" She looked at us, smiling and shaking her head. "How about that! Here you are looking for a mulberry tree, and he's got the only one around." She laughed again and slapped the countertop.

"*Yes*," Patrick whispered fiercely as he pumped his fist in the air.

My stomach lurched a little. So there *was* a mulberry tree nearby, dang it!

"Did he say he'd call us?" Patrick asked eagerly.

Her face fell. "Oh. I was getting to that. I tried to get him to take your number—even got out a pad of paper for him. But he said no thanks and left. Sorry about that."

Patrick made a noise like he'd been punched in the stomach. Meanwhile, I was suddenly feeling much better.

I looked at the lady and smiled. I wondered if my teeth looked really white to her. "Thank you for showing him our sign," I said in my politest voice. I foot-nudged Patrick. I mean, it wasn't the lady's fault that the guy hadn't taken my number, and Patrick should show some appreciation.

"Yeah, thanks," he muttered.

Green teeth grinned at us. She said, "I'll leave the sign up a while longer. Maybe something else will turn up."

We walked for a few moments in silence. Patrick's head was down, and he was hunched over. I felt bad for him—I mean, I was glad the guy hadn't taken my number, because that was one more obstacle to the silkworm project, but I hated seeing Patrick so disappointed.

"Patrick, don't forget, Mr. Maxwell is going to ask

around for us," I said. "He's a farmer—he must have a lot of farmer friends. Maybe one of them will know about a tree."

I was starting to feel like a secret agent working undercover—thinking one thing while acting and saying the opposite. It was getting a little confusing. When I said that, it almost made me hope that Mr. Maxwell *would* be able to find us a tree, and I had to remind myself that what I really wanted was no tree.

"Yeah, maybe," Patrick said, his head still down. "But we're losing time, Jules. We won't see Mr. Maxwell again until next Tuesday. There's gotta be another way. . . ."

He stopped walking and grabbed my arm so suddenly that I sort of got jerked backward. It hurt a little. "Monday!" he exclaimed.

"What about Monday?" I said crossly, pulling my arm away from him.

"He goes there on Monday mornings! She even told us the time, ten-thirty! If we're there when he's there—if we could talk to him ourselves—"

Stay calm, I told myself. Think fast. This was

what a secret agent must feel like, having to think up stuff on the spot. "Haven't you forgotten something?" I said. "It's a great idea, except for one thing. We're both a little busy on Mondays at ten-thirty, remember? It's called *school*."

Neither of us ever cut school. For me, it was mostly a matter of fear—fear of death, because my parents would kill me if they caught me skipping class. And it would never have occurred to Patrick to cut school; that was just the way he was.

"Oh. Right. Well, do we have a Monday off anytime soon?"

I shook my head. "Not for ages." Our spring break had been two weeks ago, and we were in that long stretch with no holidays at all. "Memorial Day, I think." The end of *May*. Almost two months away.

Agent J. Song, cool as a cucumber.

"Maybe I could get my mom's permission to miss one period," Patrick said. "Or maybe *your* mom could even go talk to him for us. We could ask her."

Patrick turned around and stared at the gas station. A car had just parked in front of one of the pumps. The driver got out and started filling his tank.

Patrick stared like he'd never seen anyone pump gas before.

Then he was running back to the station and calling to me over his shoulder.

"The *car!*" he shouted. "He comes in every week —that means he lives around here—we might be able to find him—"

I ran after him. By the time I caught up, he had already talked to the gas station lady and was on his way back toward me.

Grinning.

"A Ford LTD," Patrick said. "Green chassis, darker green vinyl top. From the *seventies,* Jules. That's really old. There can't be many of them around."

Patrick was already on the job, looking at every car on the street. "We might as well start searching," he said. "If we haven't found him by the end of the week, we'll ask about getting out of school."

I looked at the houses. And the sidewalk, and the grass, and the bushes.

I did not look at the cars.

Me: *I like the idea of being a secret agent.*

Ms. Park: *Me, too. I've always liked spy movies and spy books.*

Me: *So did you plan it in advance?*

Ms. Park: *No. This is a good example of what I was talking about before. You don't want to do the project, but you don't want to let Patrick know that, and it occurred to me that you're living kind of a double life, which means you're acting like a secret agent. It was the story itself that gave me the idea. Get it?*

Me: *Sort of. So do you know how my story is going to end yet?*

Ms. Park: *Not really. Everything is happening as we go along.*

Me: *Sheesh. That doesn't sound like very good planning to me. You're lucky I started talking to you—you need all the help you can get!*

Ms. Park: *I don't want to be rude, but I feel I need to remind you that I've written stories before, and the characters never talked to me.*

Me: *Well, this story is like a project, isn't it? We're doing a project together, so the ideas should come from both of us.*

Ms. Park: *Not just you and me, remember. Patrick has had lots of good ideas that have gone into the story. So has your mom. And even Kenny.*

Me (snorts): *Kenny—yeah, right. Like he could be any help.*

SIX

PATRICK WAS SURE we had enough clues to find the car. I was equally sure we'd never find it—which was what I was hoping, of course.

"Hardly anybody drives a car that old, Jules," Patrick said. "The thing is, usually we go around and don't *notice* cars. I mean, for all we know, the guy drives past us every day on the way to school! All we have to do is keep our eyes open."

I was about to ask what an LTD looked like, but Patrick was in excited mode—he plowed right over me. "He's an old guy, right? So he's probably retired. Which means"—he snapped his fingers—"the car's at home most of the time. We'll probably spot it in a driveway somewhere."

"What if he keeps it in a garage?" I said. "With the door closed. We wouldn't be able to see it."

Patrick said I was being a big pessimist. I said he was being totally unrealistic. When we got to my house, we did our homework together as usual—more exponents—but we were both pretty quiet until he went home.

I knew he was still upset with me when he left because he didn't stop in the kitchen for his bite of kimchee.

"Green. Two-tone. Old Ford. Got it." My dad and I were finishing up in the kitchen, and he was repeating what I'd just told him about the car. "I'll keep my eye out for it."

"Thanks, Dad," I said with a sigh.

My dad dried his hands on a dishtowel. "There's a guy at work who's really into old cars," he said. "I don't know if he likes Fords or not, but I'll ask him. These old-car people sometimes keep in touch with each other."

"Okay," I said. I was still being Agent Song. I'd be able to tell Patrick I'd asked my dad for help about the car, so it would seem like I was doing my best. Then maybe he wouldn't be so mad at me.

The phone rang. I ran to get it, hoping it was Patrick. We probably wouldn't apologize to each other, but if we had a normal conversation, it would mean everything was all right.

"Hello?" I said.

"Hello there." The little prick of hope I'd felt disappeared—it wasn't Patrick's voice. A man—probably someone from my dad's work. "My name is Cal Dixon, and I'm trying to reach a young lady name of Julia."

I didn't know anyone named Cal Dixon. I didn't recognize his voice, either; he spoke in a polite, old-fashioned kind of way, with a little bit of a southern accent. Cal Dixon . . . there was something familiar about the name. . . .

"This—this is Julia speaking."

"Hello, Julia. I hear tell from Miss Mona down at the filling station that you're in need of a mulberry tree."

Dixon! That's why the name had sounded familiar! The gas station lady had said, "Mr. Dixon comes in on Mondays" or something like that.

Cal Dixon was the Mulberry Man!

But he hadn't taken my number with him! Wasn't that what she'd said? How could he be calling me? What was I going to say to him?

And along with all of these thoughts at the front of my mind, there was another, smaller thought somewhere at the back of it. The gas station lady had been so nice to us, and we hadn't even asked her name. Miss Mona. I promised myself I'd call her that the next time I saw her.

"Julia? You still there?"

"Yes—yes, sir, sorry. I'm still here."

"Good. Miss Mona says you need my tree for a project, is that right?"

"Yes, sir. But not a school project. A project for a club I'm in."

"Mmm-hmm. Well, I might be willing to help you

out there, but I'd like to meet you first. Would you care to come by my place sometime this week?"

I was getting over the shock of figuring out who Mr. Dixon was, and my brain was starting to work again. I was talking to a man with a mulberry tree. This was good news for our silkworm project—which meant it was bad news for me.

Stay calm. Think fast.

I could tell him we didn't need his tree anymore. And I didn't *have* to tell Patrick about this call. Unless he asked me straight out—and why would he? Mr. Dixon hadn't taken my number, so we weren't expecting him to call — I wouldn't have to lie.

A perfect execution of my plan. No mulberry tree, no silkworm project.

Except . . .

Except for two things. The first was, what if Patrick *did* end up finding Mr. Dixon's car and his house and his tree? Then Patrick would figure out I hadn't told him about the call. He'd be really mad at me for not telling him, and double mad because of the time we'd wasted. And Mr. Dixon would think I was a complete idiot.

The second thing was harder to think through because I didn't want to think about it. But I couldn't stop my brain from trying anyway.

I'd helped make the flyers. That was a fact, plain and simple. It didn't matter that I didn't really want to find a tree. Now Mr. Dixon was inviting me to his house because of those flyers, and it wasn't fair to him when he'd gone to the trouble of calling me — it almost was like making a promise in public, and not keeping it. . . .

Mr. Dixon cleared his throat a little. I guess I'd been quiet for too long again. "Tomorrow afternoon would be fine," he said. "Would that suit you?"

Say something, Agent Song. Anything. Stall for time. "Um, sir?" I said. It came out a little squeaky. "Sir, it isn't just me, it's my friend, too. We're doing the project together. My friend Patrick."

"Teamwork," Mr. Dixon said. "That's fine. But you go on now and ask your momma or your daddy. I need to make sure it's all right by them."

Gak. Somehow I'd ended up saying yes by saying hardly anything at all.

"Yes, sir. I'll go right now."

I went into the living room. "Mom, it's Mr. Dixon. He has a mulberry tree—he saw one of our flyers. He says we can go over to his house tomorrow if it's all right with you—"

My mom nodded. "Tell him I'll be coming with you."

"Oh, *Mom*," I groaned.

She lowered her chin at me. "Julia, you are not going to a stranger's house by yourself."

"I won't be alone. I'll be with Patrick."

She shook her head. "If you want to go, I'm going with you. That's final."

So I went back to Mr. Dixon on the phone and told him it would be me and Patrick and my mom coming over.

"That's fine," he said again. "Tomorrow around four o'clock or so? I'm at 157 Grant Street. Off Orchard Drive, back of the school."

"One fifty-seven Grant Street," I repeated. "Four o'clock would be perfect, sir. Thank you."

"Bye for now, Julia," he said. "See you tomorrow."

I hung up.

Agent Song reporting: MISSION FAILURE. NEW ORDERS REQUESTED.

"One fifty-seven," Patrick said, peering out the car window. "One forty-six . . . one forty-eight . . . it must be on the next block."

"And on my side of the street," I said.

Now that meeting Mr. Dixon was unavoidable, I figured we might as well get it over with. I'd check everything out and be on the lookout for the next snag.

It was me and Patrick and my mom in the car. No Snotbrain, thank goodness. My mom had arranged for Kenny to have a play date while she took us to Mr. Dixon's.

Grant Street was only about half a mile from my house, on the other side of the school. The neighborhood didn't have rows of townhouses like ours; instead, it was mostly small homes, with a few apartment blocks mixed in.

"One fifty-seven—there it is," I said. A smallish brown house.

I was surprised to realize I was feeling a little excited. It was kind of like a treasure hunt, only instead of a chest of gold coins or something like that, our treasure was a mulberry tree.

Well, not exactly. *Patrick's* treasure was the tree. For me, it was more like Agent Song having to locate and reconnoiter the enemy's headquarters before being able to carry out orders. My new orders were to find some way to avoid getting leaves from Mr. Dixon's tree.

My mom pulled up in front of the house. There in the driveway was the green LTD. It was old, all right—a big, old-fashioned car. But in good shape. No rust anywhere.

No tree, either.

We went up the short front walk. Patrick and I sort of hung back and let my mom ring the doorbell.

The door opened.

I stared for what I hoped was only a nanosecond, then snapped my mouth shut quickly and looked at my mom.

Mr. Dixon was black.

My mom didn't like black people.

. . .

Plainfield was mostly white. Some black kids went to my school, but not very many. I didn't have any close friends who were black. It wasn't like there were big problems or anything; the kids were all friendly with each other, in class and after school and on sports teams, but the black kids pretty much hung out together in one group.

My favorite teacher ever ever *ever* was black. Two years ago I'd had Mrs. Roberts for fifth grade. She was the kind of teacher who made you wish you could have her every year for the rest of your life. She was really funny, and we never knew when she was going to say something that would crack us up, so we always listened when she was talking. And I guess because we were listening we learned stuff along the way.

She'd call on someone who had their hand raised, and if they got the answer right, she'd say something like, "Uh-*huh,* girlfriend!" And when she explained an assignment, she'd say, "We clear here? I said, *Are we clear?*" And we had to say all together, "*Crystal!*" I sometimes heard the black kids in school talk to each other like that, but I never heard any other black grownup talk the way she did. I loved it, because it made me feel like she was really being herself with us.

My mom never liked Mrs. Roberts.

It was a hard thing to learn. I mean, hard in two ways. First, it was hard because it took a long time to sink in. When I got home from school, my mom would quiz me. Not the usual "How was school today?" Instead, she asked question after question; it seemed like she wanted a minute-by-minute account of what I'd done all day long.

A little at a time, my brain put it together: She wasn't really asking about *me*. She was asking about Mrs. Roberts. I got so sick of all the questions every day that I finally asked her straight out. "How come you ask me so many questions about Mrs. Roberts?"

We were in the car, on the way to the store or something.

"Do I?" my mom said.

I hated that. I hate it when grownups answer a question with another question.

"Oh, come on, Mom. You know you do."

My mom pressed her lips together. She didn't look

at me. She kept looking at the road, even though we were stopped at a red light. "Honey, there are some things that might be hard for you to understand," she said.

"Try me," I said. "I'm not a baby anymore."

My mom nodded, still not looking at me. "Okay," she said. "You know that black people in this country have had a tough time."

"Yeah, okay."

"And lots of them haven't had the same opportunities as white people."

"Right."

"So I'm just making sure that your teacher has had enough opportunities and experience to be a good teacher for you."

She made it sound very reasonable, but it still didn't make sense. I shook my head. "I keep telling you she's the best teacher I've ever had. You've seen my tests, I'm doing fine—she's teaching me everything I'm supposed to know. Why won't you believe me?"

My mom didn't say anything for a minute. Then she smiled a little. "Okay. I believe you."

But she still didn't look at me.

. . .

So I sort of figured it out: My mom thought Mrs. Roberts might not be a good teacher, because she was black. That made things hard in a different way. Most of the time, my mom was a very nice person. I hated thinking of her as someone who might be prejudiced against black people.

I finally told Patrick about it. He didn't say anything for a minute, but I could tell he was thinking.

"Soldiers," he said at last.

"Huh?"

"The Korean War. That was when the army got integrated for the first time, and black and white soldiers fought together. I read about it."

His military-history phase, last summer. He had read a ton of books. Sometimes he read aloud to me. I was glad when he moved on to reading about crows.

"The only black people in Korea back then were American soldiers," he went on. "Maybe your mom is sort of scared of black people because they make her think of war and battles and stuff."

That seemed like a good guess. After dinner that night, I talked to my dad.

"Dad, are there black people in Korea?"

My dad looked surprised at the question. "Yes, of course there are. But not very many—almost everyone in Korea is Korean." He smiled and went on, "It was very interesting for me when I first came to the States—I never knew people came in so many different colors!"

He said it like it was a wonderful thing.

"Did you know any black people when you were little?" I asked.

"I didn't really *know* any, no," he said. "But I did meet a few. I remember the first one I ever met—a soldier. He gave me some gum." He smiled again.

So Patrick was right about the soldiers. And my dad didn't seem to care what color people were, as long as they were nice. But my mom . . . Well, maybe she'd been unlucky and had never met a *nice* soldier.

In a way, it didn't matter.

As we stood there on Mr. Dixon's front stoop,

I wasn't thinking, *Why doesn't my mom like black people?*

I was thinking, *Uh-oh. What's going to happen now?*

Me: *Whew. You're throwing a lot of stuff at me.*

Ms. Park: *Sorry. I didn't mean to. In fact, when I started writing that chapter I thought Mr. Dixon was white. I didn't realize he was black until I heard him talking on the phone. I know you couldn't tell then, but somehow he let me know that he was black. Believe me, I was as surprised as you were.*

Me: *How come he gets to tell you what to write and I don't? Is it because he's a grownup?*

Ms. Park: *Of course not. You're not being fair —I did let you tell me what to do before. With Kenny. Have you forgotten already?*

Me: *That was only a little thing. When are you going to let me decide something big?*

Ms. Park: *Be careful what you wish for.*

Me: *What's that supposed to mean?*

Ms. Park: *You'll find out.*

Me: *I hate it when grownups say that.*

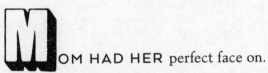

SEVEN

OM HAD HER perfect face on.

That's what I call it. Perfect—as in no expression. Perfectly smooth. Perfectly bland. My dad also has a perfect face. My parents wear their perfect faces when they don't want people to know what they're thinking.

"Mr. Dixon." My mom's voice was perfect, too.

"Yes?" Mr. Dixon looked a little puzzled. He had short gray hair and was about the same height as my dad, sort of average height for a man.

Nobody said anything for a second. It felt like a year to me.

"I'm Julia," I burst out. "You called me yesterday. Miss Mona at the gas station—"

"Oh! Of course, of course. Excuse me. Excuse my manners—I was just—I wasn't expecting—"

Finally, a crack in my mother's perfect face: Her eyebrows went up a little. "I'm sorry, you weren't expecting us? I thought Julia said today—"

"No, no, that's not what I meant." He smiled and shook his head. "I beg your pardon. It's just that when I talked to this young lady on the phone"—he nodded at me—"I was expecting white people."

My mouth fell open. I wanted to laugh, even though there was nothing really funny about what he'd said. Here I'd been thinking he was a white guy, and I hadn't said anything one way or the other to my mom, but I was sure she assumed he was white, too, and then he turned out to be black, and there he was thinking *we* would be white, but we were Asian, except for Patrick—

It *was* funny, wasn't it?

"Pardon me," Mr. Dixon said again, and held the door open. "Please come in. You're here about my mulberry tree, aren't you?"

We stood in Mr. Dixon's backyard. There was only one tree in it, at the side near the fence. Not quite as tall as his two-story house, the tree had rough gray bark and little green leaves that were just beginning to uncurl.

In other words, it looked like any old tree.

I was a tiny bit disappointed. And then I felt stupid for feeling disappointed—for pete's sake, what had I expected, gold leaves and silver bark and rubies for berries?

"It was here when I moved in fifteen years ago," Mr. Dixon said. "But nobody had taken care of it, so it was pretty scrawny. Looked more like a bush than a tree—they get that way if you don't prune them."

Aha! That explained the song!

"I trimmed it up a bit, and it's been doing just fine. Gives me a good crop every year." He looked at me and Patrick. "Either of you ever tasted mulberry ice cream?"

"No, sir," I said, and Patrick shook his head.

Mr. Dixon smiled. "Best ice cream in the world. But what was it—you want the leaves, not the berries?"

"Yes, sir," I said. "We're doing a silkworm project, and we need the leaves for food—"

"Silkworm food," Patrick broke in. "It's the only thing they eat. And mulberry trees are kind of rare around here. So far, yours is the only one we've heard of."

Mr. Dixon nodded, then looked thoughtful. "Silkworms, hmm. Sounds interesting, very interesting." He pronounced all the syllables in "interesting" but sort of skipped the first *t*, so it sounded like "inner-resting."

"I'd like to help you out," he said. "I'm just wondering—are you going to need a lot of leaves? See, if you're going to be stripping the branches bare, it might not be good for the tree."

Agent Song on the alert! "We wouldn't want to hurt your tree," I said. I looked at Patrick. "I bet they eat a lot, those worms."

Patrick shook his head and shrugged at the same

time. "I haven't done enough research yet to know," he said, looking embarrassed.

My mom cleared her throat. "They won't be needing that many, Mr. Dixon," she said. Still her perfect voice. "I helped raise silkworms when I was a girl. I used to pick the leaves from the lower branches, without bothering the rest of the tree."

Dang it—why'd she have to say that?

Mr. Dixon nodded again. "Sounds like it wouldn't do any harm," he said.

"The only thing is . . ." My mom paused and pressed her lips together for a second before she went on. "The worms will need very fresh leaves, and they'll need them twice a day. Which means the children would have to come over here quite often. For around three weeks or so. That might be an inconvenience for you."

"We wouldn't want to inconvenience you," I said. Very polite of me.

Patrick looked at me like I was nuts.

"Well, to be honest, ma'am, that's part of the reason I wanted to meet Julia and her friend," Mr. Dixon said. "Kids these days, you can't be too careful."

Now it was my mom's turn to nod. "I can understand that," she said.

"But I don't see any problem here," Mr. Dixon
said. "They look like good kids to me. They can just
come right through the back gate and get their leaves
—shouldn't be any bother."

"Thanks, Mr. Dixon!" Patrick almost shouted.

"Yes, thank you, sir," I said. What else could I say?

For now I just had to go along with things.
Withdraw and regroup, Agent Song. Come up with
another plan later. . . .

Mr. Dixon walked over to the tree and examined
the leaves on one of the branches. "They're mighty
small right now," he said.

"Oh, we don't need any today, sir," Patrick said.
"We have to order the eggs first. It'll be a while before
we're ready for any leaves."

"Why don't I take your number, Mr. Dixon," my
mom said, getting a pen out of her purse. "Julia can
call you before she and Patrick come over for the first
time."

That reminded me of something.

"Mr. Dixon?" I said.

"Yes, Miss Julia?"

I felt my face get a little hot, but there was something I really did want to know. "Miss Mona said—she told us you didn't write down my number. At the gas station. How come you called — I mean, how'd you get the number?"

Mr. Dixon chuckled. "Oh, that. Just a little game I play. I saw your sign, and I memorized the number instead of writing it down. I use little tricks. Like with yours, the last four numbers are 2139. Two plus one equals three, and three times three is nine—that's how I remembered it."

"Cool!" Patrick said.

Mr. Dixon tipped his head toward Patrick. "Sometimes I make a picture in my head—whatever the numbers make me think of. Helps keep my mind sharp, young man. At my age I need all the help I can get with that."

We left a few minutes later, Mr. Dixon's phone number safe in my pocket. In the car, Patrick asked to see it. He looked at the paper for a few seconds, handed it back to me, and then stared out the window.

I knew what he was doing. He was trying to memorize it.

As soon as we got back to my house, Patrick went straight to the computer and started typing out a letter.

"What are you doing?" I asked.

"Ordering the silkworm eggs," he answered. "Now that we've found the leaves, we can get started."

Patrick used my address on the letter and had us both sign it. "Okay," he said, "all we need now is the money." Suddenly, he was very busy folding the letter so he didn't have to look at me.

Patrick hardly ever had any money. His parents didn't give their kids any allowance until high school. He earned a little by mowing lawns (summer), raking leaves (fall), and shoveling snow (winter), and sometimes he got money for his birthday (July) and Christmas. But he was always brokest in the spring.

My family wasn't rich or anything—not like Emily's family, who lived in a big house with an in-ground pool and went on a fancy vacation every school break. But I did get an allowance, ten dollars a month, and I also babysat for two families on our street. I almost always had more money than Patrick did.

He got embarrassed about it sometimes. Like if we wanted to see a movie and he didn't have any money, I'd offer to buy his ticket, and he'd only agree to go if we called it a loan. He always paid me back. Sometimes it took him a while—last year we went to a movie in March and he couldn't pay me back until lawn-mowing season—but he never forgot.

"How much do we need?" I asked.

"The eggs are only ten bucks," he said, "but the shipping is expensive—they mail them express. Altogether we have to send in twenty-two dollars."

Wow. That was a lot.

I had twelve dollars in my money box. I was pretty sure my mom would lend me ten bucks—I had two babysitting jobs coming up in the next few weeks plus my April allowance, and I'd be able to pay her back. And I knew Patrick would give me his half of the money when he could.

But to use up all I had . . . *and* go into debt . . . for a project I didn't even want to do?

No way, I said to myself.

And then it hit me.

If we couldn't buy the eggs, that would be the end of things.

No eggs, no silkworm project.

It wasn't like with the mulberry tree, where there had always been another thing for me to worry about — Mr. Maxwell might know someone with a tree, Patrick might find the green car. . . . This was the perfect solution — absolute and final.

Agent Song going in for the kill.

I cleared my throat. "I only have twelve dollars," I said.

Patrick's face went red.

Talk about an awkward silence.

There was no way he could come up with his share on short notice. He hardly ever asked his parents for money; with all those kids, they were always hard up. And if I didn't offer to borrow the rest from my mom, he'd never ask me to do it.

"Um, I guess we have to put off sending this for a while," Patrick mumbled. "I'll just—I'll hang on to it for now." He took the letter and went upstairs, probably to put it in his backpack. Then he came down again.

"I'd better go," he said, still not looking at me. "I should help Gram with the kids." He left.

Second day in a row without his bite of kimchee.

At dinner, Kenny buried a piece of kimchee in my rice when I got up to refill my water glass. I found it right away, but I didn't say anything. I just took it out of the rice and put it off to the side of my plate.

Kenny looked surprised that I didn't make a fuss. He started to chant, "Julia doesn't like kimchee, Julia doesn't like kimchee." He took a big piece of kimchee, tilted his head back, dangled it over his open mouth, and dropped it in. "Mmm," he said. "It's *so* good." He chewed noisily with his mouth open. Disgusting. Honestly, he really did have snot for brains.

But I didn't pay any attention to him. All I could think about was what had happened with Patrick that afternoon. I finished eating and helped my dad clean up, then went to my room and sat on my bed thinking.

The more I thought, the madder I got.

I hadn't lied to Patrick. I hadn't! I really *did* have only twelve dollars. And that was more than half of what we needed, and the other half was his responsibility, and it wasn't my fault he didn't have the money!

It didn't matter that I was secretly against the project. It was like when you got a dumb present from someone. You didn't say, "What a dumb present." You said something like, "Cool! Thanks!"—so the other person wouldn't feel bad.

It was the same kind of thing: me acting like I wanted to do the silkworm project when really I didn't.

Wasn't it?

Me: *What are you doing to me? That was the worst chapter yet!*

Ms. Park: *Calm down, would you? We can't have a good conversation with you carrying on like that.*

Me: *You have to rewrite that last chapter. I hate it, I hate it!*

Ms. Park: *Hold on there. You want to get out of doing the silkworm project, don't you? This is the perfect solution — no eggs, no project. I would think you'd be pleased.*

Me: *I do want to get out of the project! But there's gotta be another way!*

Ms. Park: *If you think of anything, just let me know.*

Me: *That's great, just great. You get to do the easy parts and leave the hard stuff to me.*

Ms. Park: *Don't say I didn't warn you. You*

wanted to decide something big. Now here's your chance.

Me: *I didn't mean something like this!*

Ms. Park: *Picky, picky, picky.*

Me: *You—you—just wait. I'll get you for this—*

EIGHT

PATRICK PICKED ME up for school as usual the next morning. But things were still weird between us, and we hardly said anything the whole way there. We were having a science test that day, and he didn't even suggest that we quiz each other on the Animal Kingdom as we walked.

Patrick and I were on parallel tracks at school, which meant we had the same teachers and books and homework and everything. But we had only one class together—tech class, last period.

Science was first period. I took the test and was

relieved that I knew most of the answers. I'd been worried about it, because I hadn't studied with Patrick the night before.

It was lucky for me that I got the test over with right away, because after that things started to go crazy. No, that wasn't right—everything was normal. I was the one that was going crazy.

Second period, social studies. The currencies of South America. Lots of pesos—Argentina, Chile, Uruguay. Reals in Brazil. Bolivianos in Bolivia.

Third period, math. Story problems. Sam makes three dollars an hour and works ten hours a week. Joe makes five dollars an hour but works only three hours a week. If Sam makes three hundred dollars, how many weeks does Joe have to work to make the same amount?

Fourth period, lunch. Three quarters for change. No Connecticut, of course.

I was starting to feel really paranoid.

Everything was about money.

Every period had something in it that reminded me of what I'd done to Patrick. I felt more and more guilty as the day went on. I had to keep telling myself that I was only being fair to expect him to pay for half, that I hadn't lied to him.

Thank goodness for English class. We were reading and discussing a book about a girl named Karana, who gets stuck by herself on this island where she has to make everything she needs to survive — her own little house, her own fishing stuff, her own clothes out of skins and feathers . . .

. . . which meant she didn't need any money.

Gak! Even the classes that didn't have anything to do with money were making me think of money!

By the time tech class came around, I felt almost panicky. I'd have to use money to pay for stuff *for the rest of my life*. Every time I thought of money I'd be reminded of what had happened.

I was going to feel guilty forever.

I got to class and sat down and started clicking and typing right away so I could pretend not to notice when Patrick came into the room.

We were learning to build a website, and the day's lesson was how to put an e-mail link on your site. I got mine to work almost right away. Mrs. Moran went around helping the kids who were having trouble, so that left me free to think some more.

Why did my mom have to bring up the idea of a silkworm project in the first place? Why did Patrick have to go and get so excited? Why did he just plunge right into everything and not even bother to ask me what I thought? Why couldn't it have been some other idea that got him all fired up? Why couldn't Mr. Maxwell have been less enthusiastic about it? Why did Mr. Dixon have to have a mulberry tree? It was like a whole bunch of people were conspiring against me, and I'd been forced to come up with a plot to fight them.

But in a corner of my brain, I knew that what I was doing *wasn't* the same as telling someone you liked their present when you didn't. Because with the dumb-present scenario, you were trying to make the other person feel good.

And what I was doing was making Patrick feel *bad*.

Really bad.

It was almost as if I'd chanted at him: "Patrick never has money, Patrick never has money. . . ." In my head I could hear a nasty voice saying that over and over.

My voice.

I crossed my arms and pressed them over my stomach. Then I leaned sideways the tiniest bit so I could see Patrick, across from me at the other bank of computers. I could see only the back of his head, but it made me feel even worse.

I'd humiliated him. On purpose.

What a lousy thing to do to a friend.

All because the silkworm project was too Korean.

But Patrick didn't seem to think so. Neither did Mr. Maxwell. If *they* didn't think it was too Korean . . . maybe it wasn't.

Maybe I was wrong.

No. I was right. It was a weird Korean project, that was for sure.

Another thing for sure: I was no good at being a secret agent. Acting one thing while thinking the opposite—I'd thought it was getting easier. Sometimes it had even been fun, coming up with the right thing to say on the spot without giving myself away.

But now this, hurting Patrick—this was no fun at all.

And I had to fix it.

I opened my e-mail program and started typing.

From: Songgirl@ezmail.com
To: Patrick345@ezmail.com
Date: Thursday, March 29, 2:12 PM
Subject: Wiggle project

duh what was I thinking I can get an advance from my mom on my next allowance that will give us enough $$ you can pay me back whenever

luv J

I hit Send, then leaned over again to look at the back of Patrick's head. I didn't have to wait very long.

He spun around in his chair and looked at me. I gave him a little nod. He didn't smile, but he nodded back and gave me a thumbs-up.

I went back to staring at my screen and let out a big breath. It was like a tight knot inside me had loosened up.

Top Secret Message to Headquarters: AGENT SONG NO LONGER AVAILABLE FOR EVASIVE

TACTICS. HAS ALREADY REPORTED FOR HER
NEXT ASSIGNMENT—PROJECT MULBERRY.

On our way home from school, Patrick said, "I still
have the letter. We can send it today."

"Okay," I said. And that was all.

I gave my mom the twelve dollars and asked her if
she'd advance me my April allowance. She gave us a
check for the total. Patrick and I walked to the corner
mailbox to send off the order.

"I can't wait till they get here," Patrick said as
he pulled open the mailbox's mouth and fed it the
envelope.

"Well, we've got a lot to do while we're waiting," I
said.

Patrick had been to the library the week before
to check out silkworm books. He'd found only two.
One was for younger kids; it was mostly about the
silkworm life cycle and had lots of photos. The other
was a really old book written for people who wanted
to set up silk factories. It looked almost impossible
to read—tiny print and lots of technical stuff—but
Patrick was determined to get through it. He'd left

the picture book at my house and told me I should read it.

It wasn't like everything had changed all of a sudden: I still wasn't crazy about doing a silkworm project. But I'd made my decision—that it was worth doing to keep things good between Patrick and me —and now I had to make the best of it.

At least I was really and truly interested in the sewing part.

So we agreed that while we were waiting for the eggs, Patrick would do more research on silkworms, and I'd practice my embroidery.

My mom taught me two more stitches: outline stitch and satin stitch.

Outline stitch was exactly that—you used it to make outlines. Outline stitch was *hard*. It was hard to get the stitches to come out as a nice line on both sides. It looked best if I took little tiny stitches, but that was frustrating: I'd work and work for, like, half an hour, until my neck was all cramped from being bent over, and I'd end up with a line that wasn't even an inch long.

Satin stitch was the most important of all the

stitches, because you used it to fill in spaces. Which meant that *most* of the stitches you put in to make a picture were satin stitches. Satin stitch was more fun in one way because you got to take bigger stitches. But it also had its bad side: I had to be sure to pull the thread through *exactly* right. Too tight and the fabric would bunch up underneath. Too loose and the stitch would sag.

At the beginning I'd ask my mom to check my work. She thought I was doing pretty well, but she always pointed out little mistakes—my stitches weren't exactly the same size, or I hadn't lined them up perfectly. "Anyone can stick a needle in and out," she said. "If you want to get really good at embroidery, it's the little things that count. Because all those little things go together, to make the big picture."

Embroidering for me was mostly *un*-embroidering. I'd take five stitches, look at my work, turn it over, and look at the other side—and I'd have to pick out the last two and do them over. But the funny thing was, I didn't really mind.

It was weird, because normally I hated having

to do things over. I hated having to rewrite a home-work assignment. Or when I was younger and the Snotbrain-Maelstrom trashed something I'd built and I had to make it again.

It was different with embroidery. I got so it would bug me when a stitch wasn't just right, and I was *glad* to take it out and fix it.

When I wasn't embroidering, I was drawing little sketches. I was trying to decide what my embroidery project would be—what I would stitch once I had our very own homemade silk thread.

I was in my room before bed one night sketch-ing. My mom's embroidered flowers were so pretty —maybe I should do flowers. I drew a flower, five petals on top of a stem.

Bo-o-o-ring.

I tried drawing more flowers—rose, daffodil, tulip. Still boring. I went back to the five-petaled flower and drew it a few more times, making the pet-als different shapes. Round in one sketch, then oval, then long and skinny, then triangles . . . That one looked sort of like a star.

I guess thinking about the star distracted me, because then I started drawing stars. The kind where your pencil never leaves the paper.

Then I tried drawing just the outline, without any of those inside lines. Much harder. I drew four of them in a row, all lopsided.

I started to draw another one, and for some reason—maybe because I'd drawn them all in a row—I wondered how many stars were in each row on the American flag. Not something I was going to look up, but maybe the next time I saw a flag . . .

Flag?

Flag!

That was how I could make the project more American! I could use the thread we made to embroider an American flag!

I jumped off my bed and ran to find my mom. She was in the bathroom, brushing her teeth.

"Mom, after we make the thread, could we dye it? I need three colors—wait, the thread will already be white, right? So really I only need two—red and blue. I want to embroider an American flag—do they sell the kind of dye we'd need? Like, the stuff you use for tie-dyeing? I don't think it would be that hard—"

Sheesh. I sounded like Patrick when he gets excited. I saw my mom's face in the mirror, her mouth full of white foam.

"Jush a minute," she said. She spat and rinsed and put her toothbrush away. Then she turned to face me. "I'm sure dyeing the thread is possible, but I don't have any experience with that. My grandmother just made the thread, then she sent it off somewhere to get dyed and made into cloth, so we never did that part."

"Oh." I thought for a second. "But that doesn't mean we couldn't try."

"No, but there's something else. An American flag would be really difficult to embroider, especially if you want to make it a good size."

"I was thinking, like half a piece of paper, that size?" I said.

"Okay. The stripes are basically long skinny rect-angles, right?" My mom drew stripes in the air with her fingers. "That's one of the most difficult shapes to embroider well." She shook her head. "Definitely not something I'd recommend for beginners."

Dang it!

"I'll practice a lot," I said.

"Julia, please. You need to consider something smaller. That's why flowers look nice in embroidery —the petals are small, the leaves are small. Satin stitches look much better when they don't have to cover so much space."

Double dang it!

My mom picked up a sponge and started wiping down the sink. "Don't worry, sweetheart. I'm sure you'll think of something clever."

I went back to my room a little discouraged. But not *too* discouraged, because I still thought I was onto something. It didn't have to be the flag, but the embroidery part could be really American, and that would balance out the Koreanness of the silkworm part.

In fact, the more I thought about it, the more I realized that maybe the flag wasn't such a great idea after all. Because it wasn't very . . . creative. I mean, it wasn't something I'd designed by myself. If

I embroidered the flag, I'd be sewing a design that someone else had made up.

Sigh. I had more thinking to do.

Meanwhile, Patrick was *full* of ideas. On the way to and from school he hardly ever stopped talking.

"Jules, listen to this. We could borrow a video camera. And once the eggs come, we'll set everything up and film them every day—for, like, thirty seconds or a minute or so. And we'll have everything on tape, from the time they're tiny eggs all the way to the end, but it will be like time-lapse photography, in one film."

"Wow," I said. "That's a *great* idea."

"We can take still photographs, too. And put them together into, like, an album. So we can show people what we did even if there isn't a TV handy."

Things really started to move after that. Mr. Maxwell arranged for us to borrow one of the community center's camcorders. Patrick got permission to use his dad's regular camera. My dad moved our barbecue down to the basement so we'd have room to keep the silkworms on the back porch. He also brought up an old aquarium—he'd kept tropical fish for a hobby when he was a bachelor—which was where the worms would live.

Mr. Maxwell gave us some scraps of lumber from his farm, and Patrick's parents donated an old bent window screen. I spent the next Wiggle meeting making a frame out of the wood and stapling the screen in place to make a lid for the aquarium, so the worms would have plenty of air but not be able to escape.

Mr. Dixon's phone number was pinned to my bulletin board, but Patrick said we wouldn't need it; he had the number memorized.

"It's 555-5088," he'd told me. (A whole bunch of times.) "Fifty for the number of states—states-and-eights, it all rhymes, get it?"

We were ready. The only thing we needed was the eggs.

Me: *I'm feeling a little better.*

Ms. Park: *Glad to hear it.*

Me: *Told you I could fix things.*

Ms. Park: *But now you have to do the project.*

Me: *I know, I know. And I still think it's too Korean. But I'm getting some ideas on how I can fix that, too.*

Ms. Park: *So I noticed. In fact, that whole flag thing was your idea. What I mean is, while I was working on that scene when you were drawing and doodling, I tried my very hardest to be you. I even took a pencil and started drawing flowers, and then stars. I don't know if the flag idea would have come up if I hadn't been imagining I was you.*

Me: *So it's like even though I'm part of your imagination, I'm my own person, too?*

Ms. Park: *Yes. That's for sure. You think I'd deliberately invent a character who was as much trouble as you are?*

Me: *Me, trouble? Oh, please. Kenny, now, he's trouble.*

Ms. Park: *Kenny does not keep me awake at night talking my ear off.*

Me: *Yeah, well, at least I leave you alone in the bathroom now.*

NINE

PATRICK FIGURED THAT our order would take two or three days to get to the company, and their website said they shipped in a week to ten days. So it would be around two weeks before we'd get the eggs.

It was *exactly* two weeks.

Kenny was waiting on the front walk when we got back from another Wiggle meeting. He started yelling as soon as he saw us turn the corner onto our street.

"Julia! The worms came today! The worms are here!"

Patrick beat me to the door by two steps. We charged into the house with the Snotbrain right behind us.

"Let me see! I wanna see!" Kenny yelled.

The package was on the kitchen table. It was a square cardboard box about the size of a cantaloupe.

My mom came over to watch. I let Patrick open the parcel while I stood guard between him and Kenny. The Snotbrain could destroy the eggs in a split second if I wasn't careful.

Inside the box were a million of those foam peanuts. Patrick dug through them very, very carefully. He pulled out a little square foam block taped across the middle.

"Here," he said as he held it out to me. He was using his fingertips, like it was really fragile. "You open it."

That was nice of him, I thought. I pulled off the tape; now I could separate the foam square into two halves. Snuggled in between was a clear plastic tube — sort of like a tiny test tube. It had a cap on it.

I held the tube so Patrick could see it. The eggs inside looked like tiny dark seeds.

"None of them have hatched yet," Patrick said, sounding relieved.

Kenny pulled on my arm. "Julia, Julia, lemme see!"

"Kenny! Quit it!" I jerked my arm away from him.

"Kenny, here," Patrick said. "I'll show you, but you have to promise not to touch."

Not possible, I thought, and I was about to say so, but just then Kenny put his hands behind his back. "I won't. I won't touch, I just wanna see."

Patrick took the tube from me and held it lower so Kenny could see it. Kenny frowned. "Those aren't worms," he said.

What a dope. "Duh," I said. "They're *eggs.* They have to hatch into worms."

Patrick put the tube back into the box. "We have to keep them in the refrigerator for now," he said. "We can't take them out until we have food for them."

The first thing Patrick did after we stored the eggs safely in the fridge was to read the brochure that came with the package. It said that you could pick the mulberry leaves and store them in a plastic bag in the refrigerator for up to five days. "So we won't need to go over to Mr. Dixon's every day," he said. "We can get five days' worth at a time."

"How many leaves is that?" I asked.

"It changes," he said. "When they're first hatched, they're so tiny they hardly eat anything. The bigger they get, the more they eat. We'll just have to figure it out as we go along."

It was time to call Mr. Dixon.

"States-and-eights," Patrick said with a grin.

Mr. Dixon said to come over anytime. He also said we didn't have to ring the bell; we could just walk through the back gate and get the leaves whenever we needed them. He said it was okay even if he wasn't home.

My mom talked to me after I hung up the phone. I explained the arrangement to her.

"Good," she said. "Just get what you need without a fuss, okay? I don't want you bothering him."

Her perfect face.

Maybe she really did want to make sure we didn't disturb Mr. Dixon.

Or maybe she just didn't want us spending much time with him.

I hoped it was the first reason, but because of her perfect face, I wasn't sure.

I hated not being sure.

We decided to take fifteen leaves the first time—three leaves a day for five days. "After five days, the leaves won't be fresh anymore," Patrick said. "The caterpillars don't drink, they get water by eating the leaves, so dried-up leaves aren't any good."

Everything went fine at Mr. Dixon's house. We made sure to take only a few leaves from any one branch, and we were out the gate again in a few minutes. We didn't see Mr. Dixon. I was a little disappointed. I liked his accent.

Back home, we took out three leaves and stored the rest in the lettuce drawer of the fridge. The brochure that came with the worms said to use petri dishes, but we didn't have any. My mom gave us a shallow glass bowl that she didn't use much anymore.

I sprayed water on a coffee filter with my mom's plant mister. I put the damp paper in the bowl, then put the three leaves on top of the paper. That was what the instructions in the brochure said to do, even though the leaves wouldn't get eaten until the eggs hatched. Maybe putting the eggs on the leaves made them feel more like they were out in nature.

Patrick took out the tube that held the eggs. He uncapped the tube and poured the eggs onto the leaves. They were too tiny to count, but there were definitely more than twenty-five.

"I guess they give you extra," Patrick said.

We put the bowl into the aquarium, and I lowered its screen lid. "They won't be able to crawl for a while after they hatch," Patrick said. "They'll be too weak at first. But we might as well get into the habit of using the screen, because sooner or later they *might* be able to crawl out."

I jiggled the lid a little to make sure it was secure. Then we both bent down so we could see through the glass.

The aquarium looked pretty empty. Just the bowl at the bottom of it, with the leaves and the piece of paper in it. You could barely see the eggs.

It didn't look like much.

It certainly didn't look like an impressive project.

Patrick must have been thinking the same thing, but he was excited anyway. "This is great," he said. "This will be great on tape. It doesn't look like anything now, so there'll be a *big* difference later on."

He jumped to his feet. "I'm going to set up the camcorder," he said. "No, wait. There's something we have to do first. Jules, get Kenny."

"What?" I exclaimed. "Patrick, are you crazy? We have to keep him as far away from here as we can!"

Mars would be good, I thought. If only we could send Kenny to Mars until our project was finished. Then I realized that if Agent Song were still on the job, she'd love the idea of letting Kenny wreck the project.

But Agent Song wasn't in the picture anymore. And even if I still wasn't crazy about the worm project, I needed it to work so I could do the embroidery.

I was starting to think that it would actually be

pretty cool to make our own thread and sew something with it. Mr. Maxwell had told us about one project where a girl made a sweater from the wool of a sheep she'd raised. But somebody else had spun the wool into yarn. Maybe making the thread ourselves would impress the judges.

So we had to keep the worms safe. Especially, safe from Kenny.

Patrick grinned. "Trust me," he said.

Kenny came out onto the porch.

"Kenny, we need your help," Patrick said.

I was about to say something when he glared at me. Patrick didn't glare at me very often, so I decided to keep quiet and hear what he had to say. At least for now.

"You know those eggs," he said to Kenny. "They're going to hatch."

Kenny bobbed his head up and down. "I know, I know."

"Well, cold weather is very dangerous for them. It's spring now, but sometimes it still gets cold. If it ever gets *too* cold, they'll die."

Patrick pointed to the thermometer that my dad had hung outside the door. "You almost always get home from school earlier than me and Julia, right? Would you do us a favor? Would you check the thermometer every day when you get home? If the red line ever gets here"—he put his finger on the mark that pointed to 50°—"you gotta tell your mom. Right away. So she can move the aquarium into the house."

He looked at Kenny solemnly. "Kenny, it could be a matter of life and death. Even, like, fifteen minutes in the cold could kill them."

Kenny nodded. His face was very serious. "I won't forget. I'll check every day, I promise."

I said, "Don't you ever try to move the aquarium yourself, Snotbrain. It's way too heavy for you."

Patrick flapped his hand impatiently. "Jules, don't worry about that. Kenny wouldn't do anything to hurt them."

Had Patrick lost his mind? Had he forgotten the millions of times we'd had to redo something Kenny had ruined?

"Yeah, Julia. I'm not *stupid*, you know," Kenny

said. He shook his head and looked at Patrick like they were buddies—the two of them against me.

"Thanks, pal," Patrick said. "We're counting on you."

Kenny grinned. Then he said, "I could write it down every day. What the temperature is when I get home. That way you could tell by looking at the numbers if it's getting colder."

What a dumb idea. Like there was no such thing as the Weather Channel.

"That's a great idea!" Patrick said. "Why don't you go and get a pad and a pencil, and we'll keep them right here on the porch for you to use."

Kenny disappeared into the house on his mission. I could hardly wait until the door closed behind him.

But Patrick rushed right in before I could say anything. "Jules, trust me, this will work. If he feels like he's part of the project, he won't wreck it. Besides, I've been keeping my stuff here for ages, and he never bothers it. He only messes with *your* stuff—that's why I wanted him to feel like it was him and me together on this."

I didn't say anything at first. I was thinking.

Reverse psychology, that's what it was. Patrick was using reverse psychology on Kenny. To keep him away from the project, we'd let him get close to it.

Scary. Because if it didn't work . . .

"Okay," I said at last. "I trust you fine. It's *him* I don't trust. If you're sure this will work—I just hope we don't regret it." Then I thought of something else. "Patrick, how come you don't do this kind of thing with *your* little brothers? I mean, it's like you've given up at your house—you just bring everything over here."

Patrick sighed. "It's different when there are three of them," he said. "I'm just way too outnumbered. Besides, it's weird with little brothers—I guess it's easier to be nice to someone else's."

Patrick tied the pencil and pad together and hung them from a nail on the wall. The string was long so Kenny could reach them easily. "I'm gonna get started right away," Kenny said. He stared at the thermometer hard, then said, "Sixty-one. It's sixty-one degrees today." He wrote it down and held out the pad so Patrick could see it.

"Good job," Patrick said. "Okay, we're done for today."

We went inside. Patrick got out the brochure again. "Six to twenty days," he said. "That's what it says—our eggs will hatch sometime from six to twenty days after we get them."

Twenty days! That was nearly three weeks! "I hope it's six," I said.

It wasn't, of course.

I checked the eggs at least four times a day. When I got up in the morning. When I got home from school. After dinner. Before bed. And sometimes in between those times as well.

Nothing was happening. The eggs looked exactly the same as when we'd first gotten them—gray with a tiny black dot inside. The dots looked like periods.

Patrick had been videotaping every day, but on day six he stopped. "All the tape so far will look exactly the same," he said. "I'm gonna wait until something happens before I film again."

Kenny's numbers already filled up the first few pages of the little pad because he wrote so big. By day eleven, there was still no change in the eggs.

"Maybe they're duds," I said to Patrick. "Maybe we should write to the company and tell them."

Patrick looked worried, too, but he shook his head. "Not yet, Jules. We have to wait until at least day twenty-one."

On day fifteen, Kenny was waiting for us on the front walk again.

"You guys—come see!" he screeched.

We dropped our backpacks at the door and pounded through the house to the back porch.

When I first looked, everything seemed the same. Glass dish. Three leaves. No worms.

But then I looked closer.

The little black periods had changed into commas. "See? See?" Kenny said. "They look different, don't they?"

"They sure do," Patrick said. He grinned at me and then chucked Kenny on top of his head. "Good job, kid." Kenny grinned back at him. "Time to film them."

We got the camcorder and the tripod from the hall closet. On the porch floor there were three X's made of duct tape—one X for each leg of the tripod.

The first time Patrick had set up the camera, he'd had me make those X's so we would always put the tripod in exactly the same place.

He put the camera on the tripod, focused it carefully, then looked up at me. "Quiet on the set," he said, only half joking.

I looked at my watch. *Three, two, one*—I held up the right number of fingers while I mouthed the countdown and then pointed at him, meaning "Go." Patrick pushed the Record button. After exactly thirty seconds, I held up my hand for "Stop," and Patrick stopped the tape. Then he went and got his dad's camera, which we also kept in the closet, and took three photos of the eggs.

Everything was going according to plan. But still, all we had were eggs. When were we going to have worms?

Me: *Pssst. PSSST!*

Ms. Park: *What? Oh, it's you. Not now. I can't talk right now.*

Me: *Why not?*

Ms. Park: *I'm about to give a talk to an auditorium full of students. I have to focus.*

Me: *But this is important!*

Ms. Park: *Julia, please! I want to give a really good talk to these kids, and I can't afford to have you distracting me. GO AWAY.*

Me: *Okay. I'll go away if you do just one thing. Write this down: Cycle.*

Ms. Park: *Why?*

Me: *Because it will remind me later—what I want to talk to you about. Something that should go into the story. It's brilliant. You're going to love it.*

Ms. Park: *I don't have anything to write on*

—wait, here's a napkin. "Cycle." Got it. Now will you leave me alone?

Me: *Put it in your purse, right now. If you don't, you'll forget it.*

Ms. Park: *Oh, for heaven's sake! Okay, I'm putting it in my purse. Now get out of here!*

Me: *Just one more thing.*

Ms. Park: *Gak. What is it?*

Me: *Sheesh. Good luck on your talk.*

TEN

EVERY DAY WE put three new leaves in the aquarium and threw away the old ones. Every fifth day we went to Mr. Dixon's house and got fifteen more leaves. So far we'd been there three times and taken a total of forty-five leaves, and not a single one of them had even been nibbled on by a silkworm.

The fourth time we went, which was right after we filmed the commas, Mr. Dixon was in his yard. He hadn't been there any of the other times. He was kneeling by the back fence with a trowel in one hand.

"Good afternoon," he said as we came through the back gate. He waved the trowel at us.

"Hi, Mr. Dixon," Patrick said.

"Hi, Mr. Dixon," I said. "How are you today?"

"I'm just fine, thank you. How about yourselves?"

"We're good," I said.

"How's the project going?" he asked.

Patrick and I exchanged glances. "It's going fine," Patrick said. "We're making progress."

It wasn't a lie. Commas were progress compared to periods.

"My leaves helping any?"

"They sure are," Patrick said at the same time that I said, "Yes, sir."

That wasn't a lie, either. Without the leaves the aquarium would have looked *really* empty.

"Good. Glad to hear it." Mr. Dixon put the trowel down next to a garden fork on the ground. "Come over here, young man, if you wouldn't mind."

Patrick trotted over. Mr. Dixon held out one hand to him and put the other on the fence. Patrick braced himself, and Mr. Dixon heaved to his feet.

"Don't mind the weeding," he said. "It's the

getting up and down that's a trial for me. I'm almost ready to put in my tomato plants."

Mr. Dixon had been working on a strip of ground that ran along the fence. About half of it was nice black dirt. The other half still needed to be dug up and weeded.

"We could weed for you," Patrick suggested.

I looked at Patrick and nodded. It would be a nice way to thank Mr. Dixon for the leaves.

"That would be right neighborly of you," Mr. Dixon said. "Tell you what. You weed for a little while and I'll go inside and fix us a snack. How's that sound?"

Patrick was already on his knees with the trowel. "Sounds great, Mr. Dixon!" he said.

I took up the fork. "You dig the weeds," I said. "I'll follow you and break all the clods."

Patrick tossed the weeds onto the pile Mr. Dixon had already started. I bashed at the clods of dirt with the fork. With the two of us working together, it didn't take long to finish the strip. I liked raking the dirt with the fork to make everything nice and smooth.

It was strange, because I hated working in our yard at home. Maybe doing yard work was like being nice to a little brother—easier if it was someone else's.

Mr. Dixon came out with a tray. He set it down on the patio table by the door, then walked over to where we were working.

"Nice job," he said. "I thank you most sincerely."

I loved the way he talked. It would have sounded funny if anyone else said it, but with the way he drawled, the words seemed just right.

"You're welcome," I said. "It's our pleasure." Now, that was weird—I never would have said that to anyone else.

"Why don't you go on into the kitchen and wash up," Mr. Dixon said. "Then we'll have our snack."

The snack turned out to be tall glasses of lemonade and brownies. Homemade brownies. While we were eating, we had a nice chat. We told him about the Wiggle Club and our project. He told us some things about himself: He'd worked in a Great Values store for most of his life. His wife had died of cancer,

but he had two daughters and a son and seven grandchildren who all lived in other states, and now that he
was retired he did a lot of volunteer work.

Patrick reached for a second brownie.

"You like those?" Mr. Dixon asked.

"Yes, sir!" Patrick said. "They're the best brownies
I ever had."

He wasn't just being polite. The brownies were
awesome—very fudgy, with chocolate chips *and*
chocolate frosting.

"I'm handy in the kitchen," Mr. Dixon said. "Always
was, ever since I was about your age. Gardening and
cooking. That's what I like to do."

I looked down into my lemonade. Something he'd
just said—what was it?—reminded me of something.

Just then Patrick exclaimed, "Mr. Titus!"

I laughed. "I was thinking the exact same thing,"
I said.

Mr. Titus was a character in a book. Patrick had
read the book and really liked it, and he pestered me
until I read it, too. The book was about the adven-
tures of four kids who lived in a big old house out in

the country, and one of their neighbors was a man named Mr. Titus who liked cooking and gardening.

We both looked over at Mr. Dixon. He didn't ask us what we were talking about. He looked like he was just waiting—either we'd tell him or it was none of his business and we'd move on to something else.

I was liking him more and more.

"Mr. Titus is a guy in a book," Patrick explained. "You remind us of him—he liked to cook and work in his garden the way you do."

Mr. Dixon tipped his head a little. "Well, now. Is he a hero or a villain in the story?"

"Oh, he's definitely a hero, sir," I said, and Patrick nodded. Mr. Titus wasn't the main character in the book, but he was a really good friend to the main characters and helped them a lot.

"In that case, I'm right pleased," Mr. Dixon said and sort of raised his glass to us.

I drank the last of my lemonade. As I tipped up the glass, I caught sight of my watch. "Patrick, we better get going," I said. We hadn't told my mom we'd be gone this long.

Patrick looked longingly at the brownies that were still on the plate. Mr. Dixon chuckled. "Why don't you take one for the road," he said.

"Thanks!" Patrick took one eagerly.

"What about you, young lady."

I was already full, after that big glass of lemonade and two brownies, and I wondered whether taking a third would seem greedy, or if *not* taking one would hurt his feelings. I decided to take one. Mr. Dixon seemed pleased when I did.

At the gate I turned back so quickly that Patrick almost crashed into me.

"Patrick! We didn't get any leaves!"

"Yikes!" Patrick said. "Here, hold this." He handed me his brownie and ran back to the tree.

"Wouldn't want you to forget those now, would we," Mr. Dixon said. He waited with me at the gate until Patrick was finished picking, then waved goodbye.

I looked back as we turned the corner and saw him still standing there, watching and smiling as we walked away.

Kenny was out front again when we got home. I was feeling so good about our afternoon that I gave him my brownie.

He squashed it into his mouth in two bites. It was disgusting. And then he brushed past me and got chocolate all over the arm of my sweater.

"Kenny! You snotbrain!" I yelled.

My mom must have heard me because just then she came to the front door. "Julia Lee Song, you get into the house *this minute*," she said.

Uh-oh. I was *really* in trouble. I knew that immediately, because she used my whole name and because she wasn't yelling. She was using her special quiet extra-extra-angry voice.

"I'd better go now," Patrick mumbled. "I'll call you later." He handed me the little bundle of leaves and headed off toward his house.

My mom pushed the door open, then stepped back with her arms crossed. "You told me you were going to get leaves," she said. "That was almost *two hours* ago. Where have you been all this time?"

"Mom, I'm sorry. We did get the leaves—see?"
I held them up. "We were at Mr. Dixon's house the
whole time. We helped him do some weeding, and he
gave us something to eat, and I lost track of time. I
should have called—"

"Yes, you should have! No, I take that back. You
shouldn't have stayed so long in the first place! Didn't
you know I'd be worried? And besides, I thought I
made it clear that I didn't want you two bothering
him."

"Mom! We weren't bothering him! I told you—
we were *helping* him. In his yard. And then he gave us
brownies—"

"Julia, there's no excuse. You do *not* disappear
for two hours without me having any idea where you
are. From now on, you are to go to his house to get
the leaves and be back within twenty minutes. Is that
clear?"

She was being *so* unfair. First of all, she *had*
known where we were. We were right where we'd said
we'd be—at Mr. Dixon's house. Second, she wasn't
listening. Twice now she'd stopped me when I was
trying to explain. And third—

"I said, *Is that clear*, young lady?"

"Yes," I muttered.

She spun around and walked into the kitchen. I stood there for a second longer, then went upstairs to my room. I closed the door and sat down on my bed.

Third was something I couldn't stop myself from thinking.

Third was, *Would she be this mad at me if Mr. Dixon was white?*

By suppertime my mom had calmed down, and I had, too. Mostly, anyway. I could understand—a little— why she'd gotten so mad, and I knew I should have phoned to let her know we were staying longer than usual. So everything at supper was back to normal.

Except . . .

Except that I couldn't get *third* out of my head.

The thing was, I knew I couldn't bring myself to go up to my mom and say, "Hi, Mom, what's for dinner? And by the way, I've been wondering—are you racist?"

I was pretty sure my mom didn't think she was. I

could sort of guess what her answer might be—that of course she wasn't racist, that there were good and bad people of all colors, that you had to be careful these days and strangers could be dangerous. . . .

She'd be right about a lot of that. But wasn't everyone a stranger before you met them and got to know them?

Maybe I was being a coward. Maybe I didn't want to ask my mom because if it turned out she *was* racist, what could I do about it?

The worry stayed with me all evening and for a couple of days afterward. Not that I was thinking about it every second, but it kept popping up even though I wanted to forget it. It was like the time I accidentally bit the inside of my cheek and it got really sore, and after that I couldn't seem to stop biting the same spot a whole bunch of times more, when all I wanted to do was to keep from biting it. It took ages to get better.

Fortunately, it did not take ages before something happened that pushed *third* right out of my head. It took only two days.

· · ·

Day seventeen was a Sunday. I slept in a little; when I got out of bed, the clock said eight fifty-seven. I did the usual: washed up, got dressed, went downstairs, and checked on the eggs. The commas had been uncurling over the past few days. Last night some of them had looked like little rings — a black outline with a clear center.

I lifted the screen lid and peered inside. There were a whole bunch of tiny black hairs on the leaves — how the heck had hairs gotten in there?

Kenny . . . Had Kenny put hairs in the aquarium, maybe thinking the worms could use the hairs to make nests? What an idiot — they weren't *birds*.

But it was weird because these weren't like hairs you'd pull out of a hairbrush. They were much too short and tiny. Where had he gotten them? And what was he doing messing with the aquarium? If he'd done anything bad to the eggs, I'd — I'd think of the very worst thing I could possibly do to him and then do something *worse* than that.

I put the lid down, leaning it against my leg, reached in to brush away the hairs—and froze with my hand an inch above the glass bowl.

Because I thought I saw the hairs *moving*.

I blinked, then stared for a few seconds. The hairs were so tiny that I almost couldn't tell—were they moving? Yes—yes, there they went again, tiny, tiny wiggles. . . .

Wiggles.

They weren't hairs.

They were worms.

Little tiny itsy-bitsy worms!

Our eggs had hatched!

I hopped up and down, forgetting that the lid was leaning against my leg. It crashed down and landed on my bare foot. Which hurt, but I was too excited to really notice. Still, the pain calmed me down a little. I picked up the lid and put it carefully, carefully, back on the aquarium, so I wouldn't bump or jar it and scare the poor little things. I took one last look through the glass, then ran inside to call Patrick.

I swear he was on the back porch almost before I'd hung up the phone. With a major case of bed-head, and his sneakers untied and a jacket on over his T-shirt and sweatpants, which was what he wore for pajamas.

I lifted the lid again. Patrick sort of leaned back, like he didn't want to get in my way. Then he squatted down so he could look through the glass.

"Wow," he said in a quiet voice. "They're so little! They're almost—well, you wouldn't really say they're cute, would you? But they're the littlest worms I ever saw."

"It's like they're barely *there*," I said. "I can't believe they're going to become big huge caterpillars."

Patrick had shown me pictures on the Internet. The worms were supposed to grow to be as big as a person's finger.

We saw that there weren't any rings in the eggs anymore—all of the eggs had hatched. "They'll need to eat within a day," Patrick said. "They'll be too weak to eat much at first, but from now on we'll have to keep a really close eye on them. And on the leaves

—we have to make sure there are always fresh ones in there."

Patrick went inside and came back with three fresh leaves. He handed them to me. "Okay, Jules," he said. "You have to get them onto the new leaves somehow."

I picked up one of the old leaves, using my fingertips to hold just the very edges. The worms were so tiny that their wiggling didn't really get them anywhere.

I held the old leaf right over a new one, tilted it, and gave it a very gentle shake. Nothing happened.

The worms were either hanging on for dear life or they were somehow stuck to the leaf.

I put the leaf down carefully. Patrick frowned. "Maybe you need to pick them up and move them," he said.

"They're too tiny," I said. "My fingers are so fat compared to them—I'm scared I might crush them. Do you wanna try?"

Patrick took a step back. "No way," he said.

What we needed was something like tweezers. But

even tweezers were scary—I still might squash them. Something tiny, that wouldn't squeeze them . . .

I went into the house and up to my room. My mom had given me a basket to keep my sewing stuff in. I pawed through it until I found my pincushion and took it back down to the porch.

"I'm going to try this," I said, holding up a long pin. It had a bead on the end of it.

I took out one of the leaves with the worms on it and told Patrick to take out a fresh one, and to put the lid back on the aquarium. We put both leaves down on top of the screen. Now I wouldn't have to bend over so far.

I held the pin tightly with the bead pushing against my palm, which helped me keep the tip steady. I put the pinpoint down next to one of the tiny worms and slid it a millimeter at a time until it was under the worm. Then I lifted it and moved it to the fresh leaf.

"Whew," I said at the same time that Patrick said, "Good." We both let out big breaths.

It took me more than half an hour to move all the worms. I felt like a doctor doing microsurgery

—slow, gentle, careful, so I wouldn't hurt any of them.

Sheesh! They were *so* tiny. It was hard to believe anything that little could survive for long.

Me: *I've been thinking about something. It's not fair. When I mess up, everyone sees it. Like with Patrick and the money thing. But no one sees any of your mistakes. Remember when you started my whole story in present tense and then decided to change it to past tense? Nobody else saw how long it took you. Or how mad you got. I think I even heard you swear a couple of times.*

Ms. Park: *Ahem. Well —*

Me: *So I did some digging around on my own. Look what I found.*

Ms. Park: *Where did you get that?*

Me: *I found it on the hard drive. In your first-draft file.*

Ms. Park: *Put it back!*

Me: *Too late. Already copied and pasted.*

I took up the fork. "You dig up all the weeds," I said, "I'll follow you and break up all the clods."

Patrick threw the weeds onto the pile Mr. Dixon had already started. I broke up the clods of dirt with the fork.

Me: *Pretty awful stuff. Look at all those "ups" —four in a row.*

Ms. Park: *Come on. Everyone makes mistakes. I fixed that part—you can check on page 133. Besides, if you want to know the truth, I like finding my mistakes and trying to make the story better—changing little things here and there, taking some words out, choosing others. . . .*

Me: *Hmm. It's like embroidery. Only with words instead of stitches.*

Ms. Park: *I like that idea.*

Me: *Thanks. That's twice now you've admitted my ideas were good. So maybe you should go back and reconsider giving me a little sister—*

Ms. Park: *Sorry. No dice.*

ELEVEN

IT WAS AMAZING how fast our worms grew. Patrick started videotaping them twice a day. He'd come over early on the way to school to tape them, and then we'd do it again after supper. I always moved them to new leaves before we did the taping, and he'd get shots of the old leaves, too. At first the worms ate teensy nibbles, so there were only tiny holes in the leaves.

On the second day I noticed that when I picked up a worm on the pin, there was an almost invisible strand of webbing attaching it to the leaf. Maybe it had been there all the time but I hadn't been able to see it before. It was so thin that it broke as soon as I lifted the worm.

I pointed it out to Patrick.

"I think that's how they attach themselves to the leaves. So they don't fall off," Patrick said. "I mean, our leaves are always flat, but if they were on a tree out in nature, the worms would have to sort of hang on."

"Makes sense," I said. "And maybe they're also getting started practicing. To make silk."

I wondered if the worms were like dogs — if they were getting to know me by my smell. They seemed to get a little excited when I moved them; they'd squirm around more. But as soon as they were on a new leaf, they settled right down to eating again. By the fifth day they were big enough to wiggle onto a new leaf by themselves, so I didn't have to move them anymore. That was a relief. Moving them twice a day had been hard work. And when we took out the old leaves, we saw that they were always covered with strands of webbing.

The Tuesday after our worms hatched was another

Wiggle meeting. This one was a field trip. It was also our day to get more leaves from Mr. Dixon. I made sure to tell my mom that I wouldn't be home until suppertime, that after the field trip we'd be stopping by Mr. Dixon's place. She didn't say anything—just gave me a look.

"I'll come straight home," I said. "We won't stay, okay?"

I'd been trying to think of a way to make her change her mind—to get her to say it was all right for us to visit with Mr. Dixon sometimes. But I hadn't come up with a strategy yet. Until then, I planned to be very angelic about the whole thing and not get her mad all over again. That way maybe she'd be easier to convince later.

She nodded. "Have a good time on the field trip," she said.

We were going to visit Mr. Maxwell's farm. We rode in a mini-school bus, about twenty Wiggle members altogether. When we got to the farm, Mr. Maxwell had us gather around him in front of the barn.

"Most of you have been here before," he said,

"so you don't have to take the grand tour again if you don't want to. This is Tom." He raised his hand toward a man who had come out of the barn and was standing nearby. "Tom will take anyone who doesn't want to go on the tour down to the second pasture, and you can help him round up the cows."

There were only five of us who had never been to the farm before; the rest had been Wiggle members for a long time, and Mr. Maxwell did the farm field trip every year. So it was just me and Patrick and three other kids who followed Mr. Maxwell to the field he called the first pasture—the one closest to the barn.

Mr. Maxwell led us to the barbed-wire fence that enclosed the field. Inside the fence there was a flock of sheep. Some of them were eating, and others were lying down. I counted six lambs. They were adorable, little and white and fluffy.

The bigger sheep were not nearly as pretty. Their butts were really nasty-looking.

"The first thing you should know about this place is that it's what's called a 'sustainable' farm," Mr. Maxwell said. "That means we try to farm here in a way that's good for both the environment and the animals."

He gestured at the field. "I had thirty head of cattle in here until two days ago. The cows eat, right? And what happens when an organism eats?"

"It grows?" Patrick guessed. He must have been thinking about our worms.

"Yes, but what else? Something more directly connected to eating. It eats, and then—" He stopped and waited for us to answer.

"It poops?" That was a boy named Sam.

Everyone giggled. Mr. Maxwell grinned and said, "That's right, Sam—it poops! So there are the cows, pooping all over the field"—we laughed—"and all that manure is fertilizing the field."

He took a breath and went on. "Now, we can't leave the cows in there for too long—they'd eat up all the grass and erode the soil. We have to move them out. On other farms the field would just sit there, empty, while the farmer waited for it to recover, for the grass to grow thick again. But on a sustainable farm, you don't have to waste time waiting."

Mr. Maxwell made a movement with one hand,

like he was pushing something away from him. "Cows out—" he said, then made a pulling motion with his other hand "—chickens in. We'll take a look at the chicken coop later. It's on wheels. Chickens like shelter; they don't like to be out in the open all the time. With the coop here, the chickens can go in and out all day long, and we can move it around to cover the whole field."

"A mobile home for chickens," Patrick said.

"That's right," Mr. Maxwell said. "Okay, remember—I've got a field full of cow poop, right? And what happens when you have a lot of poop in one place?"

"It stinks." That was Sam again. More laughter.

"Yeah, okay. But you also get a lot of bugs. Flies, especially, right? They lay their eggs in the poop and you get lots of nice healthy maggots."

"*Eww.*" We said that all together, and Patrick added, "Yuck," and made a face as well.

"Well, wouldn't you know it—chickens *love* maggots!" Mr. Maxwell said. "So the chickens eat up the maggots, and they also scratch—they scratch at the cowpats and spread them around, and they scratch at the soil, which keeps it nice and loose and aerates it. There they are, tilling the soil and spreading the fertilizer and keeping down the pest population and saving me money on chicken feed!"

"Cool," Patrick said. I thought so, too.

"Then we move the chicken coop to another field and let the sheep in here—that's the stage we're at right now." Mr. Maxwell waved his arm at the sheep. "Now, because of all that cow manure, there are *lots* of weeds in the field. Cows won't eat weeds, but sheep will, so I don't have to use chemicals to keep the weeds down. Better for the soil, and better for the animals, too."

I watched the sheep nearest to us. Sure enough, one of them was working on a patch of what looked like thistles—purple flowers with prickly leaves. The sheep didn't seem to be bothered by the prickles.

"Then we move the cows back in here, and the whole thing starts over again. The field's been occupied the whole time, but it's not worn out and used up—it's ready for the next round."

He squatted down by the fence. "Get down low, everyone," he said. "Have a look at the grass." He reached between the fence rails and raked through the grass with his fingers.

We all got down on our knees and looked closely at the grass.

It was green. It had blades. There were patches of clover.

In other words, it was just grass.

Mr. Maxwell was watching us. He grinned when he saw our faces. "Just grass, right?" he said.

"Okay," Patrick said, "so what's so special about it?"

"It's *healthy!*" Mr. Maxwell boomed out. "It's green and thick and growing like mad, and the soil underneath is full of nitrates and other good stuff. If you were a cow, that grass would look like an ice-cream sundae!"

All of a sudden I felt like I was seeing the grass the way a cow would. It really did look quite delicious —deep and rich and juicy green, full of sweet-smelling clover.

"When you come right down to it, I'm a grass farmer," Mr. Maxwell said. "A grass and soil farmer.

That's my main job — making sure the soil stays fertile so the grass grows well. The animals do everything else, and if we all do our jobs, the system sustains itself — it keeps going and going."

"What other kind of farming is there?" Patrick asked. "Is there such a thing as non-sustainable farming?"

"Well, they don't call it that, of course," Mr. Maxwell answered. "They call it 'commercial' farming. Ever been to a chicken farm?"

We all shook our heads.

"But you've heard of battery chickens, haven't you?"

"I have," said Hannah, one of the girls in the group. "I saw a program on TV once. There were, like, hundreds of chickens in one building, and they never got to go anywhere, and they had to just sit there crowded into these little boxes and lay eggs all day long."

"That's right," Mr. Maxwell said. "And because the chickens are so crowded together, they start to fight. To keep them from hurting each other, the farmer has to snip off the ends of their beaks and the tips of their claws. Battery chickens are also more prone to disease, so the farmer has to put a lot of drugs in their feed to keep them healthy—chemicals that end up in their eggs."

Yuck. I liked eggs. I'd never thought about what went into them before.

"Chickens raised on battery farms are miserable creatures, in my opinion," Mr. Maxwell said. "Not like my chickens. My chickens get to run around and eat grass and worms and go into their coop whenever they feel like it. I like having happy chickens."

I'd never heard Mr. Maxwell talk this much before. I could tell he was really into this farming stuff.

On the way back to the barn, Patrick walked next to Mr. Maxwell and asked a bunch of questions. I didn't follow everything they said, but I did learn that commercial farming was cheaper—that it cost a lot more for Mr. Maxwell to run his farm than it did for commercial farmers to run theirs. Which meant that happy-chicken eggs were more expensive in the grocery store, which was why most people kept buying battery eggs.

That made things trickier than I'd thought. At first I'd wondered why everyone didn't farm the way Mr. Maxwell did—it seemed so sensible. But it turned out that underneath all those cool small details, there was a bigger picture that was a lot more complicated.

During the rest of the field trip, Mr. Maxwell showed us the barn and the sheepcote, where the animals stayed in the winter. We got to climb into the barn's loft and jump down onto a big pile of hay— that was a blast. We rode on a tractor. And everybody got to take a turn going into the chicken coop and finding an egg.

We got to keep the eggs, too. Mr. Maxwell gave us all cartons to put them in. I couldn't wait to eat mine—I wondered if it would taste different from a battery egg.

On the bus ride home, and then as we walked to Mr. Dixon's house, I kept thinking about that first pasture. I liked the idea of the cycle—the cows, then the chickens, then the sheep, and starting all over again. For some reason it made me think of our worms. Egg, then worm, then cocoon, then moth, and back to egg again.

Mr. Dixon was sitting outside when we got to his house.

"We can't stay long today," Patrick said. I'd told him about getting in trouble with my mom. "We have to be home in time for dinner."

"Best event of the day," Mr. Dixon said. "Wouldn't want you to miss that."

We picked twice as many leaves this time, thirty altogether. Patrick and I had talked it over, and judging by the holes in the leaves, we had guessed the worms were going to need at least five at a time starting in another day or two.

Boy, were we ever wrong. In the next two days the worms ate twenty-two leaves! They had turned into eating machines. The incredible thing was, we could actually *hear* them eating. I never would have thought that worms made noise. But ours did—*crunch crunch, munch, nibble nibble, crunch.* Even Kenny quieted down and stood still to listen.

We had to go back to Mr. Dixon's just three days

later. I was half afraid to tell my mom that, and she put on her perfect face when she said it was okay for us to go, but she didn't seem to be really mad anymore. Maybe it helped that she'd raised silkworms before and knew how much they could eat.

"Back so soon?" Mr. Dixon called when he saw us. He had a pair of garden shears in his hand and was cutting some really pretty flowers that grew against the fence. Pink and purple ones.

"Those are really nice, Mr. Dixon," I said. "What kind are they?"

"Sweet pea," he answered. He skipped the *t* again, so it came out like "swee-pee."

"Now, do you two have time for a little visit, or do you need to be running along?"

I looked down at the ground and was trying to think of what to say when Patrick answered for me.

"We can't stay, Mr. Dixon. Julia's mom made us promise not to take too much of your time, so we're supposed to just get the leaves and go home right away. She—she likes to be sure where we are all the time."

Mr. Dixon nodded. Then he said, "Sounds to me

like she's being a good momma. Too many kids running wild these days, and their mommas got no idea
what they're up to."

Maybe that was it. Maybe my mom was just being
a good mom. . . .

"But I'd like her to know that I surely do enjoy a
visit from young people every now and again," he went
on. "Tell you what. I got some homegrown peppers in
my freezer. From last year's crop—it's still too early for
anything this year, of course. I'd like to send a few of
them home with you. And you tell her from me that I'd
be pleased to have you stay and chat sometimes."

I looked up and smiled. "Thanks, Mr. Dixon. I'll
give her the message."

Mr. Dixon put down his shears and went into the
house with the flowers. Patrick and I got busy picking
leaves; we'd brought a plastic bag with us because we
were going to pick a lot this time. We counted fifty
leaves, and Patrick picked a few more just in case.

We finished just as Mr. Dixon came out again.
He had a bag with red peppers in it, and some sweet
peas with their stems wrapped in a damp paper towel.

My mom loved flowers. I felt hopeful—surely once

she got the flowers and the peppers, she'd know that Mr. Dixon was a nice guy, and let us stay sometimes.

Mr. Dixon handed me the bag and the flowers. "I hope she likes those peppers," he said. "They're not bell peppers—they're a different kind. A little spicy. Used to grow them when I lived down south, but they do fine up here, too, just come ripe a little later. I use them in my jambalaya. You like jambalaya?"

"I love jambalaya!" I said. My mom made it sometimes, and I'd liked it ever since I was little. Rice and seafood and chicken and sausage all jumbled up together. *Yum!* I also liked the word *jambalaya;* it was fun to say.

"Well, I reckon your momma will be able to get some good use out of them," he said. "Don't Chinese people use a lot of peppers in cooking?"

For a second I couldn't say anything. I felt my face getting hot. And then Patrick rescued me again. "Julia's not Chinese, Mr. Dixon. Her family is Korean." He started talking faster. "And her mom does cook spicy stuff, and her family eats spicy food all the time, so I'm sure she'll like the peppers a lot."

"Well, that's fine," Mr. Dixon said. "I'll see you two later then. Mind you go right on home now."

"We will," Patrick said.

We left and walked a little way. Then Patrick turned to me. "Jules," he said in a low voice, "he didn't mean anything. He said 'Chinese,' but he meant, you know, Asian. Any kind of Asian."

I nodded. "I know, Patrick. It's okay."

But it wasn't.

Once in a while somebody thinks I'm Japanese. But that's it—either Chinese or Japanese. It seems like those are the only kinds of Asians anyone has ever heard of. I didn't know exactly why it bugged me. Maybe because it made me feel like being Korean was so nothing—so not important that no one ever thought of it.

I was used to people making that mistake. I was used to having to explain that I was Korean and not Chinese or Japanese, and most of the time I didn't bother getting very upset, unless people were being mean about it.

But I'd really been surprised to hear Mr. Dixon say the same thing, and Patrick could tell.

Why? Why had I been so surprised?

Jostle, jostle, jostle. My mom had assumed things about my teacher Mrs. Roberts because she was black. Mr. Dixon assumed my family would like peppers because we were Chinese. And I assumed that Mr. Dixon—somebody black, somebody who probably had a lot of experience with racism—would never make a mistake like that.

But Mr. Dixon and I weren't thinking *bad* thoughts about each other, not like my mom had about Mrs. Roberts. We weren't being mean about it, either, like those girls who had chanted "Chinka-chinka-Chinaman" at me. That made a difference, didn't it?

Then why was I thinking all those things at the same time?

I thought again about why I didn't like people to assume I was Chinese. They thought they knew when they didn't. And because they thought they knew, they never asked.

So in a way, it didn't matter whether what you were thinking was good or bad.

Not knowing.

And not knowing—or not caring—that you didn't know.

And not bothering to find out because you didn't know you didn't know.

That was the problem.

Me: *I feel a little dizzy. Not knowing about not knowing reminds me of something—a picture in a book Patrick once showed me. There was this drawing of a can of dog food, right? And on the can there was a picture of a dog holding a can of dog food. And on that can there was a dog holding a can of dog food, and on THAT can—*

Ms. Park: *Okay, okay I get it.*

Me: *That picture made me dizzy the same way. It's, like, I want to stop thinking about it, but I can't.*

Ms. Park: *Sometimes I feel like that when I'm writing. Especially when I can't get things in the story to work the way I want them to. Things go wrong, and I can't seem to fix them, and I can't stop thinking about them. I get dizzy, too.*

Me: *So what do you do about it?*

Ms. Park: *Usually I take a little break. I might get up and putter around in the kitchen—I like to cook. Or I might take the dog for a walk.*

Me: *Does it work?*

Ms. Park: *Sometimes. Other times I just have to move on to another part of the story and fix the problem later.*

Me: *I don't have any dog to take for a walk, and I don't know how to cook yet, not really. So let's try the moving-on thing instead.*

TWELVE

PATRICK CAME OVER extra *extra* early the next morning. We had to videotape the worms as usual, and we also had a miniproject we wanted to do.

We were going to have eggs for breakfast—the two happy-chicken eggs plus two ordinary eggs. My mom was going to fry all four of them and then we'd eat them side by side to see if there was a difference in the taste.

Patrick was making a list of the differences. He wasn't writing them down, since this wasn't for school or anything—he was just saying them out loud. I was watching my mom and making toast at the same time. Kenny was still in bed; his school started later than ours. And finished earlier. No fair.

"Happy egg, brown. Battery egg, white," Patrick said.

My mom cracked the first egg—a white one—on the edge of the frying pan. Then she did the brown one.

"Two taps to crack the brown one," Patrick said. "Only one tap for the white one."

The same thing happened with the other two eggs. Patrick looked pleased. "He was right," he said.

Mr. Maxwell had told us that his eggs had sturdier shells than battery eggs.

The battery eggs spread out a lot more in the pan; their whites seemed runnier than the others'. "The brown eggs are nice and fresh," my mom said. "A fresh egg doesn't run in the pan. I remember that from my family's chickens in Korea. These eggs were laid a few days ago, right? But I bought the supermarket eggs last week, and I'm sure they were at least a few days old when I bought them."

"Happy egg, yellowy orange yolk," Patrick noted. "Battery egg, yolk paler."

That was interesting. I'd always thought of ordinary eggs as having nice yellow yolks, but the happy eggs were a much deeper color.

My mom dished up the eggs while I buttered the toast. Patrick and I sat down at the table. I saw that my mom had put Mr. Dixon's sweet peas in a vase. They looked nice. Maybe it was a good sign. . . .

"Which are you going to try first?" Patrick asked.

I thought about it. "The battery egg," I said and took a bite, making sure to get both white and yolk on my fork. Patrick did the same.

We looked at each other. "Tastes like egg," I said.

We giggled.

Now for the happy egg. I felt a little nervous as I cut into it with my fork. That was silly—it was only an egg.

We chewed and swallowed and were silent for a moment.

Patrick said, "Tastes like egg."

I laughed, but I felt a bit disappointed.

Patrick took another bite of his happy egg. "Maybe it does taste a little different," he said. "A little . . . eggier?"

My mom came over to the table. "Can I try?" I handed her my fork, and she tasted a bit of my happy egg. "Oh, yes," she said. "This egg has a lot of flavor."

I tried another bite of each egg.

Maybe there was a difference, but it definitely wasn't a *big* difference.

Patrick must have been thinking the same thing because he said, "That must be why Mr. Maxwell doesn't make much money. His eggs are more expensive, and they don't taste *that* much different. So people must figure, Why buy them?"

"Because the chickens are treated better," I said, "and maybe the eggs are better for us."

"*We* know that now," Patrick said, "because of the field trip. But how many people get to go on a field trip like that? Hardly anyone."

Hardly anyone. Still, I had been to the farm. . . .

I turned to my mom. "Mom, could we get happy eggs from now on?"

My mom was packing Kenny's lunch. He didn't like school lunch, so he always took a sandwich. "We'll see," she said.

Gak. Typical grownup answer. I was about to start trying to convince her when Patrick waved his fork at me.

"Jules, I've been thinking. You realize we're sort of running a silk farm now?"

I snorted. Our aquarium—a farm?

"No, really," Patrick said. "We're raising the caterpillars to make silk—that's what they do on a silk farm."

"Well, maybe, but it's the smallest farm in the history of ever," I said. "I don't know if you could really call it a *farm*."

"Still"—Patrick waved his fork again like he was trying to erase what I said from the air—"I was thinking that we should try to make it a sustainable farm, like Mr. Maxwell's."

"How the heck would we do that?"

Patrick put down his fork. "I don't know," he admitted. "I just thought it would be a good idea."

It *was* a good idea, and I told him so. But I still didn't see how we could do it. For a start, we didn't have any other animals we could make a cycle with.

"Keep thinking about it," Patrick said. "Maybe one of us will come up with something."

Other people might not have found the silkworms very interesting—all they did was wiggle around and eat. But I loved watching them. They were a grayish greenish white color, and big enough now that you could see all the little segments of their bodies and their tiny, delicate feet.

I also loved listening to them. The bigger they got, the louder they crunched. When they were all eating at the same time, it sounded like a miniature army marching over gravel.

Most amazing of all were their faces. I used a magnifying glass to look at them. Two eyes and a mouth—those were clear. And something in the middle, a little bump that I guess was the nose.

Their mouths were pretty mean-looking. You could see the two parts—lips? is that what you'd call them?—except instead of being top and bottom, like people lips, they were side by side and looked like pincers.

When Patrick looked through the magnifying glass, he said, "Yikes! That's nasty." He handed me back the magnifier hastily. "They look like aliens."

"Aliens!" I said, indignant.

"Yeah. Their faces. Like some kind of miniature alien monster."

Kenny agreed with him. Great buddies, those two.

I guess they were right, in a way. But sometimes things can be so ugly that they're cute, and I thought our worms were adorable. I especially loved the way they moved. They'd raise their heads up like they were looking around, then stretch themselves *waaaay* out and let go with their rear ends at the last minute, but very smoothly. It didn't look like crawling, not the way Kenny used to crawl when he was a baby. It was more like *rippling*—they rippled across the leaves.

They pooped, of course. Little tiny black pellets. Every time we cleared up the silkworm poop, it made us think of the cow poop on Mr. Maxwell's farm, and that made us wonder how we could make our project —I refused to call it a farm—sustainable.

Patrick drew Mr. Maxwell's cycle on a piece of paper. Blades of grass, cows, cowpats, flies, chickens, and sheep. He drew them so they formed a circle, with arrows in between.

Then he made another drawing of our project: a mulberry leaf with an arrow pointing to a caterpillar.

We looked at the drawings side by side. Ours looked pretty pathetic next to Mr. Maxwell's.

"There's gotta be some way we can make it a cycle," Patrick said.

I studied the drawings for a minute. "Wait," I said. "You left a couple of things out."

I took the pencil from him and drew a mulberry tree next to the leaf. Then I made a few tiny dots with the pencil point next to the caterpillar. "The tree and the poop," I said. At least our cycle didn't look quite so bare now.

"That's it!" Patrick shouted. "You did it!"

"I did?" I stared at him and then back at the drawing. "I don't get it."

Patrick took the pencil back. He drew a long arrow circling around from the caterpillar poop to the tree.

I still didn't get it.

Patrick was grinning. "Don't you see? We take the worm poop to Mr. Dixon's, and use it to fertilize his mulberry tree! It's not a big fancy cycle like Mr. Maxwell's, but it's still a cycle, and this way the worms and the tree are sustaining each other. Get it?"

Wow, was he ever smart. But I have to admit I felt pretty silly when we took the poop to Mr. Dixon's house. We cleaned out the aquarium every other day and kept the poop in a little plastic bag. By the time we went to get more leaves, we had about a handful of poop—if the hand was the size of a newborn baby's.

I said I didn't think it was enough to make one bit of difference to the tree.

"It doesn't matter," Patrick insisted. "It still counts."

He told Mr. Maxwell about it at the next Wiggle meeting. Mr. Maxwell was so pleased that he gave us high fives.

One morning when the worms were two weeks old, I went out to the porch to do my normal check on them. I looked through the aquarium's screen lid.

My heart almost stopped.

Some of the worms were just lying there. They weren't wiggling or eating.

They were dead.

My heart went from stopped to top speed in about a second. It was pounding so hard I could hardly think. Call Patrick first? Pick up the dead worms? Figure out what had happened?

I looked around wildly at Kenny's pad on the wall. The numbers had been getting bigger pretty steadily —it was getting warmer every day. The worms couldn't have frozen.

There were plenty of leaves. They hadn't starved.

What had we done wrong!

Just then Kenny bumped open the back door and came out onto the porch.

"Kenny," I said hoarsely.

"Hey, what's wrong with them?" he said, pushing his face closer to the glass.

I couldn't speak. I could feel hot tears in my eyes.

"Cool," Kenny said.

Cool? He thought the dead worms were *cool*? I was going to *kill* him.

"They're like little hollow worms," Kenny said.

What was he saying? Not that it mattered. They'd be his last words on this earth—

Wait.

What?

Hollow?

I blinked away the tears as fast as I could and lifted the lid so I could take a closer look.

He was right.

What I'd thought were dead worms were just the *skins* of worms.

Our worms were molting.

"I almost had a heart attack," I told Patrick a few minutes later. He'd come over as soon as I called.

Patrick clucked his tongue at me. "Jules, you should have known they were going to molt. It's in the book."

"I haven't read it all yet—I hadn't gotten to that part."

"They're gonna shed twice more," Patrick said. "This is their first instar."

"*What* kind of star?"

"Instar," Patrick said. "It means the stage between moltings. Let's get some pictures of these skins."

While Patrick arranged (and rearranged, and rearranged) the photos in a folder, I practiced my embroidery. By the time the worms were three weeks old, I'd had two months of practice. My mom said I was getting pretty good.

But I still hadn't decided what to embroider for the project. I wanted it to be something really special — something that would deserve genuine homemade silk thread.

Ideas were easy. *Good* ideas were hard.

My mom and I had agreed on a compromise about visiting Mr. Dixon. She said we could stay, but only for half an hour, and not every time, and of course I always had to tell her.

Maybe I'd gotten it all wrong. Maybe my mom really *was* just being a good mom, and her getting mad at me before had nothing to do with Mr. Dixon's being black.

Except . . .

Except for what she said at the very end of our conversation.

"Fine," she said. "I guess it's only fair that you visit with him a little, seeing as you're getting the leaves from him. I'm glad we've got that settled." Then she sort of shrugged. "But I have to say, I still can't quite understand it. He's an old man—what could you and Patrick possibly have in common with someone like him?"

I shrugged back at her and said, "He's nice, that's all."

Someone like him—was that sort of a coded way of saying something? Underneath what she said, did she really mean *someone black?*

Or was it just what she said—that he was an old man?

I wondered if thinking about this race stuff too much made you see it in places where it didn't exist.

But then I wondered the opposite: Maybe it existed all the time, and you only saw it if you were really thinking about it?

• • •

The silkworms got big enough for me to hold. Before, I'd been scared of hurting them. Now, they were almost as big as my pinkie. Their feet were bigger, too, which made them really look like caterpillars instead of worms.

I'd pick one up and let it crawl around on my hand. They hardly weighed anything at all; it was just a soft little tickly feeling in my palm. I *loved* holding them.

I thought I was starting to be able to tell the worms apart. They were striped at their segments, but their stripes weren't exactly the same, some wider, some narrower. There were three that looked to me to be a tiny bit bigger than the rest, and two average-sized ones that seemed the most sluggish.

I mentioned these things to Patrick.

"Oh, come on, Jules," he said. "You only *think* you can tell them apart. We'd need, like, scientific equipment to measure their differences."

He was probably right. But that didn't stop me from trying to tell them apart.

Patrick shot some tape of me holding one of the caterpillars. It cooperated beautifully — it rippled around on my palm and stood upright on its back feet and moved its head like it was looking around.

"That's great," Patrick said. "I got a really good close-up of him."

"How do you know it's a *him?* It might be a her."

"We'll be able to tell the moths apart," Patrick said. "I read about it. The females are usually lots bigger and have wider butts."

I giggled. "Moth butts."

"Well, yeah. The bottoms of their thoraxes are wider. But there's no way to tell with the caterpillars, not by just looking."

I looked more closely at the caterpillar in my hand. "Maybe we could find a way," I said. "If we did, that would make us, like, real scientists."

Patrick clicked his tongue. "Julia, entomologists have been studying caterpillars and moths, like, forever," he said. "If there were a way to tell, they'd have found it by now."

"What kind of ologist?" I said. "Oh, never mind. They're cute no matter which sex they are." I held the caterpillar out toward him. "Want to hold it?"

Patrick shook his head. *"Entomologist,"* he said.

"Entomology—the study of insects. And no, I don't want to hold it. I have to put the camera away."

"Just for a minute. It's fun, they're kind of tickly—"

"I don't like being tickled."

"C'mon, you never hold them."

"Jules, I said *no!*"

Patrick's voice was so fierce it startled me. I pulled my hand back and curled my fingers a little, sort of protecting the poor caterpillar from the loudness. "Whoa," I said. "What's with you? It's no big deal, I just thought you ought to hold one. So you can learn everything about them. You can look at them a lot closer if you hold one."

Patrick turned away. "I don't want to," he muttered.

He was being so weird. "Why not?" I persisted.

"Because."

Great answer. "Because what?"

Patrick pulled open the door with a hard jerk. "I don't want to talk about it!" he yelled, and stomped into the house.

Sheesh!

I put the caterpillar back into the aquarium, replaced the lid, and followed Patrick inside. He was putting the camcorder into the closet.

"Patrick."

He closed the closet door and turned to face me. "I'm sorry I yelled," he muttered.

"I didn't mean to make you mad, I just . . ."

He looked down at the floor. "It's not your fault," he said. "It's—well, I never told you this. But I'm—I—I've got—" He shuffled his feet and seemed to be studying his toes very hard. "I've got a thing about worms."

"What do you mean—what kind of thing?"

He sighed and looked up, but not right at me. "You know what a phobia is, right? Well, I have a worm phobia. I hate them. They give me the creeps, big time."

I looked at him in disbelief. "You have a *worm* phobia?" I said. "I can't believe it! Why the heck did you want to do this project?"

He shifted his feet again. "Well, it seemed like a really cool idea, making our own thread. I wanted an animal project, and we couldn't have any of the big ones. And I thought doing this might help me get over it—might make it so I wasn't phobic anymore."

Now he looked at me. "Besides, it wasn't just me —you wanted the project, too."

Ha! I almost laughed out loud. I guess Agent Song had been pretty good at her work after all.

But I didn't say anything about that, about not wanting to do the project before. I was still too amazed by what Patrick had just told me.

Afraid of worms! Of those sweet little tickly things we'd been raising since they were tiny eggs! *Ridiculous!* I mean, being scared of sharks or—or alligators or something big and scary, I could understand that. But worms?

"Why are you scared of them?" I asked. "They don't bite or anything! I mean, they might poop on your hand, but even their poops are no big deal." Caterpillar poop was tiny, plus it was hard and dry, not disgusting like dog poop or cowpats.

"I know all that," Patrick said, "but that's the thing with phobias. You're scared even when there's no real reason to be. I read about it on the Internet."

He straightened up a little. "I found a website that lists more than five hundred phobias. Mine is called 'scoleciphobia.' 'Phobia' means fear in Greek, and 'skolex' means worm. I memorized some of the other ones too. Amaxophobia—fear of riding in a car. Ephebiphobia—fear of teenagers. And my favorite: Arachibutyrophobia. Guess what that is?"

"Arack *what*? How the heck would I know what it is?"

"A-rach-i-bu-tyro-phobia. Fear of peanut butter sticking to the roof of your mouth."

"No way! You made that up."

"I did not! It's a real phobia."

We both laughed, and I was glad that Patrick was sounding more like himself. "So has the project helped?" I asked. "Are you less phobic now?"

He shrugged. "A little. I mean, I still don't like them. But at least I can look at them now. Before, I used to get grossed out just by the sight of them. And it helps a lot when I look at them through the camcorder. Or the camera lens. I don't know why, but it makes it easier."

"Wow," I said. We were both quiet for a moment.

I was thinking how hard it must have been for Patrick to tell me about his phobia. Boys weren't supposed to be scared of crawly things. "I'm glad you told me," I said. "I won't bother you about holding them anymore."

He nodded. "Thanks," he said. He sort of shivered and rolled his shoulders. "How about some work on South American agriculture now?"

Me: *Oh! Oh! Oh! I just figured something out!*

Ms. Park: *And what would that be?*

Me: *It's you, isn't it? You're the one with a worm phobia! No one would think of giving Patrick a phobia like that unless they had one, too. That's it, right?*

Ms. Park: *Would you please lower your voice? There's no need to shout.*

Me: *Ha! You're not answering me, which must mean I'm right!*

Ms. Park: *So how come you're all sympathetic toward Patrick but not toward me?*

Me: *Because Patrick is my friend—not someone who bosses me around all the time.*

Ms. Park: *Boss you around? Excuse me? I can't even get you to talk more quietly.*

Me: *And besides, I don't think it's fair for you to force your phobia onto poor Patrick.*

Ms. Park: *Patrick is his own person, you know. I can't help it that he's phobic.*

Me: *I'm glad you didn't make me phobic. I love those worms.*

Ms. Park: *It wouldn't have worked. You're just not the type.*

THIRTEEN

WHEN THEY WERE twenty-four days old, the caterpillars stopped eating. I didn't panic because Patrick had warned me it would happen. "They'll stop eating and change color—they'll turn yellowish," he'd said. "That means they're getting ready to spin their cocoons. Tomorrow we should move them into egg cartons."

Patrick had read that the caterpillars liked to have their own little compartments to spin in. The brochure suggested toilet-paper tubes cut in half or egg cartons. I'd saved two egg cartons, and Patrick brought over a third from his house.

There were twenty-six worms. "I'm not going to put them twelve, twelve, and two in the cartons," I said. "I think they'd like it better to be divided up more evenly. I'm going to put them eight, nine, and nine instead."

The next day we cut through the hinges of the egg cartons so the tops would be easier to take off and put back on. Patrick's research said the caterpillars liked to spin in the dark, so we'd be leaving the tops on most of the time, but we still wanted to be able to watch them once in a while.

I picked up each caterpillar carefully and let it crawl on my hand for a few seconds. Then I put it into an egg pocket.

Some of the caterpillars sort of stood up halfway and swayed around like they were investigating their new homes. Then they coiled themselves up neatly. We cleaned out the old leaves one last time and put the egg cartons into the aquarium.

Now that I knew about Patrick's phobia, I couldn't

believe I'd never noticed it before. If he wasn't shooting tape, he was fussing with the focus or playing back what he'd taped or switching to the regular camera. He *never* looked at the caterpillars straight on. The only way he ever looked at them was through a lens.

I could tell he was still really creeped out by them. I tried to think of something that scared me the same way. I didn't like spiders very much. . . . When I was little, I slept with a night-light on. . . . But I knew neither of those was really a phobia, not like Patrick's.

I couldn't imagine what it felt like, to be *that* scared of something. Sometimes I wanted to talk him out of it again, make him hold one, stuff like that. But that didn't seem fair. I just had to try to understand in other ways. Like by thinking how it was very brave of him to want to do a worm project at all. And how he'd decided to do it both to try to get over his phobia and because he thought it was what I wanted.

My best friend had a phobia. If he could deal with it, so could I.

The next morning I went to check on the caterpillars. The egg cartons wouldn't open. Somehow they had gotten stuck closed. I showed Patrick when he came over.

"I can only get them open a little," I said. "Wait, let me try again."

I held one of the cartons at eye level, pulled at the top, and managed to open it a crack so I could peek in.

"Wow!"

"What is it?" Patrick asked. "What do you see?"

"They're going nuts!" I said. "They're moving their heads around like crazy. I can't see very well, but they're all, like, frantic. Do you think something's wrong? Maybe they don't like it in there."

"No, I think they're okay," Patrick said. "The silk comes out of their mouths, and the book said they're constantly in motion while they're weaving their cocoons. That's gotta be what they're doing. But why can't you open the carton?"

"There's all this webbing. It's stuck to the top and bottom—it's like they've glued the carton shut. Maybe they want to make their cocoons in private."

"That's not it," Patrick said. "They make a little sort of hammock thing first, to hold the cocoon. And they have to string it up somehow. So they're doing it from top to bottom. They're not gluing the carton shut on purpose."

I watched for another few seconds. Then I closed the carton gently and put it back in the aquarium.

Patrick flapped his arms. "There's no way I can film through that crack," he said. "What a bummer —this would be the most interesting part."

On the way to school we talked it over some more. "There's gotta be some way to film them," Patrick kept saying.

We were in luck—it was a Friday, so we had the whole weekend to work on the problem.

First we tried cutting a window into one of the cartons. This was a little scary. I picked the carton that held eight caterpillars—I knew I'd left the corner egg pockets empty, so that was where I cut the window. I used nail scissors and poked a hole with the point, then made tiny tiny snips to cut a square. All the while I was praying that none of the caterpillars had moved into that space overnight.

I pulled out the little cardboard square and let out a huge breath. It was fine—there wasn't any caterpillar under it. But I couldn't really see any of the other ones either, unless I put my eye right up to the window and tilted the carton a little.

Patrick shook his head. "We gotta make the window bigger," he said.

So I did that next. I cut more of the carton, so three egg pockets would be exposed. But when I lifted off the flap of cardboard, a caterpillar came with it, trailing a little cloud of webbing.

Patrick jumped back in alarm.

"Oh no!" I cried out, then rescued the poor thing as it dangled in the air.

I pulled the caterpillar off the flap—the webbing was *really* sticky—and put it back into the carton. Then I checked it over anxiously. It seemed fine, but the first thing it did was try to wiggle away from the open window.

"This isn't working," I said. "See, it doesn't like being out in the open."

I ran into the house and found a roll of masking tape. Then I ran out to the porch again, taped the bits of cardboard together, and stuck them back onto the carton.

I felt much better once I'd done that. It had made me quite panicky—the caterpillar was obviously upset by our invasion of its privacy.

"Gak," Patrick said. "Now what?"

Kenny came out to the porch.

"Hey, Patrick. Hey, Julia. Whatcha doing?"

Patrick explained the problem to him.

"So you need to leave us alone," I said to Kenny and glared at him. "We have to work on this."

Kenny ignored me. The snotbrain. He looked at Patrick. "Just put one in a little jar," Kenny said. "That way you could film it through the glass."

Patrick looked at him and then at me. Then he laughed, clapped Kenny on the shoulder, and said exactly what I was thinking. "Why didn't we think of that?"

I opened the cardboard window one last time, took out the same caterpillar, and put it into a little glass jar. We'd poked air holes in the metal lid. We kept the jar in the aquarium alongside the egg cartons, and I put a cup upside down over it so it would be dark most of the time. But whenever Patrick wanted to film, we took the jar out for a few minutes.

It was *so* cool. My parents came out to see, and Patrick's parents brought Hugh-Ben-Nicky over that evening to have a look. The porch was very crowded; I worried that all those people would upset the caterpillar. But it didn't seem to care, not even when both the twins started jumping up and down and screeching with excitement.

The caterpillar moved its head constantly. Sometimes fast, sometimes a little slower, but never stopping—it looked like really hard work. The silk came out of its mouth just as Patrick had said.

At first the silk was almost invisible. You could see the strands only if you looked really hard.

By the next morning, though, the caterpillar had already wrapped itself in a layer of silk. It looked like it was living inside a cloud. We could see its black mouth moving, moving, busy, busy, busy. Patrick wanted to stay up all night to film it, but both our moms vetoed that idea. The following morning he was at our house in his pajamas again. The silk was almost solid; now we could barely see the black mouth moving inside.

I was glad Patrick was taping it; I'd be able to watch it again as many times as I wanted. But I knew it would never be as special on tape as it was now, happening right in front of me, those wispy threads at first barely more than air, and then like a cloud, the caterpillar spinning layer after layer after layer, each layer made of one hundred percent real silk thread.

I stood with a piece of paper held behind my back. "I am a genius," I said to Patrick.

It was the afternoon of the third day of the spinning, a Sunday. Patrick was sitting on the couch in our living room. I'd told him to sit there while I went and got the paper from my room. He raised his eyebrows at me but didn't say anything.

"I've decided what I'm going to embroider. I'm going to do"—I paused dramatically, then whipped out the paper—"the Life Cycle of the Silkworm."

I held up the sketch I'd drawn.

"Egg. Worm. Cocoon. Moth." I pointed to the drawings one by one. "And wait till you hear the best part. I'm going to use regular embroidery floss to do the egg and the worm. And the moth, too. But for the cocoon, I'm going to use the thread we make. The cocoon is made of silk in real life, and it will be made of silk in the picture too, get it?"

Patrick grinned, a really huge grin.

He got it, all right. I almost felt like hugging him. He put his hands up in the air and bent forward a few times like he was bowing to me.

"Julia Song, you *are* a genius. We are absolutely, positively, going to win a prize at the fair."

I made a silly curtsy back at him. "Thank you, thank you." I'd thought of doing the life cycle a while back. But it was the caterpillar that had given me the idea for the cocoon part. I'd watched it spin for a while right before I went to bed, and I'd woken up that morning with my genius plan.

I had known right away that it was perfect. There was just something so completely *right* about it. It wasn't American, like the flag—but it wasn't Korean, either.

Or maybe it was both?

Patrick took the sketch from me and studied it

for a second. Then he looked up. "It's almost like an exact picture of the whole project, right?"

I nodded. "That's what I was thinking."

"Okay, so if it's supposed to be just like the project, you should leave out the moth at the end."

"Why would I leave out the moth? That's the final stage, right?"

"The final stage of the silkworm life cycle, yeah. But not the final stage of our project."

"What are you talking about?"

"We're not going to have any moths."

"Of course we're going to have moths," I said. "Look how great they're doing—they're almost done spinning their cocoons."

"But we want thread. So you can sew with it."

"Yeah, so?" What was Patrick's problem?

Patrick rolled his eyes at me. "Oh, I get it. You never read the book, did you."

"I did so. I mean, I didn't read every word, but I looked through it. I studied the pictures a lot—I traced one for the caterpillar sketch."

"Jules. If you'd read the book you'd know."

"Patrick, *what* are you talking about?"

He shook his head. "If you want to get silk from the cocoons, you have to kill the—the creatures inside. *Before* they come out as moths."

What!

I stared at him. I could feel the blood going out of my face. "You have to *kill* them?"

Patrick nodded. "You have to boil the cocoons. For about five minutes, to dissolve all the sticky stuff that keeps them together. Then you can unwind the silk. But the boiling kills them—the pupae."

For once, there was no jostling in my head because there was only one thought, with nothing else for it to bump into.

Kill them.

We'd have to kill them.

My hands were freezing cold. I closed them into fists—open, shut, open, shut—while I tried to get my brain to work.

"Patrick, wait. Why can't we unwind the cocoons *after* the moths come out?"

"Jules. It's all in the book."

"Okay, okay. I didn't read the stupid book! Tell me!" I almost screamed.

Patrick spoke slowly, like he was trying to calm me down. "The moth gets out by making a hole in the cocoon, right? To make a hole it has to chew through the silk—well, it doesn't actually *chew*, it spits out this chemical that dissolves the silk and makes a hole. And the hole goes through *all* the layers of silk, see? So instead of one nice long thread, you'd end up with a million tiny short pieces that you couldn't sew with. Silk farmers never let the moths come out—it would ruin everything. Get it?"

I got it, all right. I closed my eyes because I felt dizzy.

I hadn't known that I didn't know.

Ms. Park: *Julia?*

(silence)

Ms. Park: *Julia, come on.*

(silence)

Ms. Park: *I know you're there. I can hear you.*

(more silence)

Ms. Park: *Okay, so you're upset. But we need to finish this story. I'll give you some time on your own now, but I'll be back in a little while.*

Ms. Park: *Julia? Three days and you haven't said a single word. You still need more time? All right, let me know when you're ready.*

Ms. Park: *Are you ready now? It's been two weeks. . . .*

Ms. Park: *Come on—you can't hide forever.*

Ms. Park: *At least I hope not.*

Ms. Park: *Julia! I've given you more than a*

month! Enough is enough! You can't run away from this—it's your story and you have to see it through! Now stop being a coward and come talk to me RIGHT THIS MINUTE!

(silence)

Ms. Park: *Julia. I'm sorry I got mad. (pause) But I really want to finish this story, and I can't do it without you. I'm stuck. Completely stuck.*

(silence continues)

Ms. Park: *There. That was what you wanted at the beginning, remember? For me to admit I'm not always the boss? Well, you were right. I need you. Talk to me.*

(silence gets louder)

Ms. Park: *Please? Please, please, PLEASE?*

FOURTEEN

JOSTLE, JOSTLE. My brain was starting to work again.

Jostle, bump. Bump, thump, jostle, bang. Bang, crash, smash into smithereens.

If we let the worms live and turn into moths, I wouldn't be able to make the picture with real silk and we wouldn't be able to enter the Domestic Arts category, so we'd only have Animal Husbandry, and even that wouldn't be very good. It would be more like a school science project than a really good Wiggle project.

Worst of all, I'd be letting Patrick down.

But for me to carry out my genius idea—to embroider the cocoon with real silkworm silk, we'd have to—

Crash, bang, smash.

I opened my eyes and looked straight at Patrick. "We can't do it," I said. "We just can't."

Patrick jumped to his feet. "Jules! Are you nuts?"

"Patrick—"

"It's such a great project! And your idea for the picture is genius—I told you that already! It's perfect! It'll be the best project ever! And with the video, and the photos . . . we've been working so hard, Jules! We can't let it all go to waste!"

I still felt dizzy, and now my stomach was starting to churn. "I know we've been working hard," I said, "but so have *they*." I nodded in the direction of the back porch. "They're spinning like crazy, Patrick. Because they think they're going to get to be moths at the end of all this."

Patrick flapped his arms wildly. He looked like an ostrich that had forgotten it couldn't fly.

"Oh, for pete's sake—they don't *think* anything! They're *worms!*"

"How do you know they don't think?" I demanded.

"Jules!" Now he raised his voice. "It's not even like they're endangered or anything! People have been making silk for ages and ages, and they always kill the worms, and nobody worries about it, and they're *fine*—there are still billions of silkworms in the world! You—you just—you're being *stupid* about this!"

Stupid? *Stupid?*

Somehow that was the last straw.

"Stop blaming me for everything!" I yelled back at him. "You're the one who's afraid of them! You probably *can't wait* to kill them! I bet that's why you picked this project—so you could kill a bunch of poor innocent caterpillars! Besides, I didn't even want to do this in the first place!"

"I'm not—What?" Patrick frowned. "What do you mean, you didn't want to do it? I thought—"

"You thought wrong! I hated the idea right from the start! But you were so—so—I knew I'd never be able to talk you out of it, so I just went along with

everything—and the money—and then your phobia
—and I'm the only one who cares about them!"

From the look on Patrick's face—a combination
of stunned and confused—I knew I wasn't making
much sense, but I couldn't stop to get organized. I
felt like any minute I might start to cry, so I kept yelling because maybe yelling would keep me from cry-
ing. "So now everything's all messed up! And it's not
fair, and it's not my fault!"

I turned and stomped up the stairs to my room.
But I didn't close the door because I wanted to hear
Patrick leaving.

He did.

He didn't come back after supper to do homework,
either. Instead, he sent me seven e-mails. I couldn't
believe it—there were way too many kids in his
house, and he hardly ever got the computer more
than once a night.

From: Patrick345@ezmail.com
To: Songgirl@ezmail.com
Date: Sunday, May 27, 6:43 PM
Subject: Wiggle project

I cant believe you think I would pick this project just to kill worms. Thats the most ridiculous thing I've ever heard. Just because a person has a phobia doesn't make them a MASS MURDERER.

From: Patrick345@ezmail.com
To: Songgirl@ezmail.com
Date: Sunday, May 27, 6:54 PM
Subject: Wiggle project (again)

its not like theyre PETS, Julia. You didnt even name them. And besides worms have NO nerve endings. They don't feel pain, it wouldn't hurt them NOT ONE BIT.
i am not lying to you about this!!!

From: Patrick345@ezmail.com
To: Songgirl@ezmail.com
Date: Sunday, May 27, 7:09 PM
Subject: Wiggle project

when theyre in the cocoons they're hibernating,
they are not even CONSCIOUS.

From: Patrick345@ezmail.com
To: Songgirl@ezmail.com
Date: Sunday, May 27, 7:11 PM
Subject: Wiggle project

scientists dont even KNOW if worms HAVE consciousness, not

like humans anyway, thats why theyre called a LOWER FORM OF LIFE!!!

From: Patrick345@ezmail.com
To: Songgirl@ezmail.com
Date: Sunday, May 27, 7:38 PM
Subject: WIGGLE PROJECT PLEASE READ AND REPLY

you kill mosquitoes dont you? ALL THE TIME. you dont worry about THEM do you??? WHY IS THIS ANY DIFFERENT?????

From: Patrick345@ezmail.com
To: Songgirl@ezmail.com
Date: Sunday, May 27, 8:23 PM
Subject: Wiggle project

ARE YOU GOING TO ANSWER ME????

From: Patrick345@ezmail.com
To: Songgirl@ezmail.com
Date: Sunday, May 27, 9:06 PM
Subject: Wiggle project

I cant believe you would do this to me. its MY PROJECT TOO AND I WANT A CHANCE TO GO TO THE STATE FAIR!

Patrick and I weren't speaking. It was the first

time this had ever happened. Sometimes I would feel bad about it, but mostly I was too angry at him. He didn't care. He could hardly even look at the caterpillars, much less hold them. It didn't matter one bit to him if they lived or died.

And, although it was hard to admit, I was mad at myself, too. If I'd read the book when he gave it to me, I'd have known what to expect. I was sure I'd still have felt bad about having to kill them, but it might have made a difference.

Somewhere along the line, winning a prize at the state fair had sort of faded from my mind. When had that happened? It was before this—before I found out about killing the worms. . . . Probably the first molting, when I'd thought they were dead. From then on I was worried about the caterpillars, and the silk, and the embroidery. But somehow I'd stopped thinking about the prize.

So Patrick was still thinking about the fair and the prize, and I wasn't. Did that make one of us right and the other one wrong?

And which was which?

• • •

I left home early so I wouldn't have to walk to school with Patrick. Not that it was hard—he was avoiding me, too. But we couldn't avoid each other at the Wiggle Club. Mr. Maxwell was meeting with everyone about their projects. I heard Patrick go up to him and ask to go last, and we waited until everyone else had left.

Mr. Maxwell must have been able to tell that something was wrong. He looked from Patrick to me and back again and said quietly, "What's up, kids?"

Neither of us said anything for a moment. Then Patrick took a deep breath and explained everything in one of the longest sentences I'd ever heard. He finished by saying, "and you need to talk to her, Mr. Maxwell, because you're a farmer and you kill stuff all the time, don't you, and it doesn't make you a bad person, so could you make her see that?"

Mr. Maxwell leaned forward with his elbows on his knees. "Julia, I know exactly how you feel," he said quietly. "I didn't grow up on a farm, either. And I'll never forget the first time I killed an animal that I'd raised myself. It was a chicken." He smiled, but it was a serious smile. "It was bloody, and messy, and I almost got sick."

He flicked a glance at Patrick. "But Patrick's right. I do kill things all the time now. Or rather, I send them off to be killed." He paused. "Remember the field trip a couple of weeks ago, those lambs in the first pasture?"

We both nodded.

"They're gone now. I sent them off to the locker —that's the place that does the slaughtering."

I swallowed hard. Those sweet fluffy lambs . . .

And I love lamb chops.

Mr. Maxwell spread out his hands in sort of a shrug. "Nowadays, most people get meat already cut up and wrapped in nice neat plastic packages. They don't really want to be reminded that it came from a living, breathing animal."

He looked at us and nodded. "I think it's important not to forget. To feel responsibility for what we eat, and to raise farm animals with respect for their lives. That's why I work the way I do. And that's also why I run the Wiggle Club. I want at least a few kids to learn some of these things, and think about them, and maybe appreciate farming a little more."

He reached out and patted me on the shoulder. "Julia, I'm sorry you're upset about your worms. But I'm also glad in a way. Not glad like hip, hip, hooray. Glad because it means you're really going to appreciate that silk. It's going to mean a lot more to you than if you didn't care."

I took a deep breath.

He'd almost changed my mind.

Almost convinced me that it wouldn't be so bad to kill our worms. The way he had to kill his chickens and his lambs.

But that last thing he'd said — "you're really going to appreciate that silk."

He was *assuming* we were going to make the silk. He wasn't trying to convince me that it was okay to kill the worms — he was only trying to make me feel better about doing it.

Patrick was looking at me, and I knew he knew me well enough to know what I was thinking.

I put on what I hoped was a perfect face. "Thanks, Mr. Maxwell," I forced myself to say. "And thanks for doing the Wiggle Club. You're right—it does make me think about things I never thought about before."

"Great," he said, and grinned. "My good deed for the day." He stood up and put his jacket back on. The three of us walked out of the building. Mr. Maxwell said goodbye and went off toward the parking lot.

I started walking toward home. On my own.

"Jules."

I walked a couple more steps. Then I stopped and turned back.

Patrick didn't try to catch up with me. He just spoke from where he was standing. "I know I'm not gonna be able to change your mind," Patrick said. "I figure we can still finish the animal part of the project. But I gotta ask you something. The other day when—when we were—well, you said you hadn't wanted to do the project in the first place. How come you never told me that?"

He wasn't going to try to change my mind anymore.

It was too much to think about all at once—so much that my mind sort of went blank for a second. But then I focused again. One thing at a time. Patrick was waiting, and he'd made the first move toward trying to fix things up between us, and he'd told me the truth about his phobia, even though it must have been hard.

So it was only fair that I should tell him the truth, too.

"It was too Korean," I said at last. "I didn't want to do the project because it seemed so, well, *foreign*. I wanted to do a really American project."

Now for the hard part. I looked down at the sidewalk in front of Patrick's feet. "So for a while I was only pretending I wanted to do it. I kept trying to find a way out of it. That's why I wouldn't ask my mom for a loan at first. I figured if we couldn't buy the silkworm eggs, that would mean no project. And we'd have to think of something else."

"Oh." Patrick shifted his feet a little.

Silence. The money stuff was still no fun to talk about.

"I'm sorry," I whispered. "I guess I should have told you at the very beginning. But you seemed so —so happy about the idea, and I didn't think I could talk you out of it."

More silence.

"Okay," he said at last. "I just wanted to know."
We didn't say anything more the whole way home.

That evening, just when I was about to shut down the computer and go to bed, I got an e-mail. From Patrick. No message, just a link to an article on a website.

It was an article about Susan B. Anthony. I knew about her—we'd studied her last year in social studies. She was famous for her work on equal rights for women in the U.S. She'd helped women get the right to vote.

Why the heck was he sending me stuff about Susan B. Anthony?

But I wasn't going to make the same mistake again. I read the article from start to finish.

It was mostly about her house somewhere in New York, and how it was a museum now, with exhibits on her life. And then I came to this paragraph:

One display shows a dress made of black silk brocade. The silk was made from worms raised by women of the Church of Jesus Christ of

Latter-day Saints in Utah, and was given to Anthony by them on the occasion of her 80th birthday. (She had the cloth made into the dress.) Susan B. Anthony said of the dress: "My pleasure in the rich brocaded silk is quadrupled because it was made by women politically equal with men. The fact that the mulberry trees grew in Utah, that the silkworms made their cocoons there, that women reeled and spun and colored and wove the silk in a free state, greatly increases its value."

So that was why he'd sent it to me.

I sat back in my chair.

Susan B. Anthony was as American as you could get.

I knew then what Patrick had done. He'd probably spent the whole rest of the afternoon and evening searching the Internet. He must have had to make a *huge* fuss to get all his brothers and sisters to let him have the computer for that long. He must have told them it was really important.

But not because he was still trying to talk me into

killing the caterpillars. He'd said he wouldn't try to convince me anymore, and I believed him.

What he was trying to do was find something that would make me feel better.

The next morning, I waited out front so we could walk to school together.

Ms. Park: *Welcome back! I'm so glad you're talking to me again! Does this mean you've decided what to do?*

Me: *No. Yes. What I mean is, I've decided that I can't decide. You're going to have to do it yourself.*

Ms. Park: *I am not going to decide this for you.*

Me: *Well, how about this then: We end the story now, right here. Without me deciding either way.*

Ms. Park: *Oh, I'm sure the readers would just love that.*

Me: *I don't care what they think.*

Ms. Park: *That's no good. You have to care about the readers. Because without them, you won't exist.*

Me: *What do you mean?*

Ms. Park: *It's like this: You exist while the story is being written — like right now — but pretty soon the story will get made into a book. And after that, it's the readers who will bring you to life.*

Me: *So . . . the story has to have an ending that readers will like?*

Ms. Park: *Well, they don't have to like the ending. But it's completely unfair not to give them one. It's like not keeping a promise. And you've already told me how much you hate that.*

FIFTEEN

THAT AFTERNOON WE got my mom's permission and went to Mr. Dixon's house to tell him that the worms had spun their cocoons and we wouldn't be needing any more leaves.

We went to the gas station first. We said hello to Miss Mona and thanked her for her help—we told her how we'd ended up getting leaves from Mr. Dixon's tree. Then we bought three rolls of wintergreen mints as a thank-you present for him.

My money, Patrick's idea. It was really thoughtful of him to come up with that.

Mr. Dixon greeted us, and we told him our project was almost finished.

"So was it a success?" he asked.

There was a little silence. Then Patrick said, "Yeah, you could say that. I mean, we learned a lot."

Mr. Dixon nodded. "Good. Glad my leaves could help. Will you be coming round again? I hope you'll stop by, time to time."

"Sure, Mr. Dixon," Patrick said. "We could bring the video once it's finished, if you'd like to see it."

"I'll look forward to that," Mr. Dixon said. He winked at us. "You two are going to make my leaves famous, isn't that right?"

We all laughed. Then Patrick and I gave him the mints. He laughed again and thanked us, then told us about the trick of eating them in front of the bathroom mirror with the door closed and the lights out, and crunching down on them hard so you could see sparks in your mouth. I'd known that from a long time ago, but I'd forgotten about it. I thought I'd buy another roll sometime and show Kenny—he'd think it was totally cool.

And then I could use the mints to bribe him when I wanted him to leave me alone.

We walked back, and Patrick went home for supper. I went out to the back porch, lifted the lid off the aquarium, and opened one of the egg cartons just a crack.

The worms had finished spinning. There were nine cocoons in that carton, each one of them a perfect oval. Egg-shaped, but smaller than chicken eggs.

I touched one gently. A nice dry shell around the little pupa inside. It was like a miracle, how worm spit could turn into something so sturdy and beautiful.

Kenny came out and stood next to me. "Can I see?" he asked.

I lifted the carton top a little more.

"Cool," he breathed.

Then he looked at me, his face serious. "Patrick told me. About killing them to get the stuff you need. But you don't want to."

I put the top back on.

"It'd be neat to see the moths come out," Kenny said.

Well, what do you know. The first person who'd said anything at all about the moths.

"Julia, do you have to kill *all* of them? Why can't you just get the stuff from some of them and let the others get to be moths?"

I'd already thought of that. But we'd still be killing them—some of them, anyway. And besides, how would I choose? It would be like playing God, to have to decide which lived and which died.

Mr. Maxwell probably had to do that. There were sheep in the pasture—adult sheep. That meant not all the lambs got slaughtered. Some of them got to live and grow up. How did he decide which ones?

"Maybe you wouldn't have to kill that many of them, Julia," Kenny said. "How much stuff do you need? Maybe just one cocoon-thingy would give you enough."

I didn't know the answer to his question. The jostling started again.

What if he was right?

What if I only needed one cocoon?

What if I only had to kill one of them?

Which one?

I needed to do some reading.

I went up to my bedroom, scrabbled around in the mess for a few minutes, and found the book Patrick had left me. Ages ago. He told me he'd renewed it twice already.

I read the table of contents, found the chapter I needed, and turned to one of the last pages.

> You can make your own thread by twisting the silk from five cocoons together. Fewer than five and your thread will be too fine. . . .

I flipped back a few pages and skimmed until I found the answer to my next question.

> The silk of each cocoon can be up to a mile long. . . .

A mile! Amazing!

Five strands of silk each a mile long, twisted together into one thread.

Way more than enough to embroider a cocoon.

If we boiled five of the cocoons, we'd have enough thread for the project. The other twenty-one pupae could become moths. And I wouldn't be letting Patrick down.

That was the big picture. It wasn't exponents. It was baby math—even Kenny could have done it.

I thought about it all the rest of that evening. Especially while I was embroidering.

I was getting pretty good at embroidery. I'd figured out a few things lately, which helped my stitching a lot. When I was doing outlines, tinier was better. Stitches so small that one by itself looked like a speck. If I kept taking tiny stitches like that, I ended up with a line that was beautifully smooth. I loved seeing how those specks, one after another after another after another, merged together into a nice unbroken line.

It took me almost an hour for just one leaf! And all that time, in between being careful about where I put the needle in and how tightly I pulled the thread, I was thinking about my darling caterpillars.

Five. (Take a stitch.)

Sacrifice five of them, and the rest could live. (Take five stitches.)

It's not a compromise. Not for the doomed five. Life and death is not something you can compromise about. (Take two stitches. Undo one and do it over.)

I want them all to live. But I also want to be able to finish our project the way we planned it. (Three more stitches.)

I want a perfect solution. (Two perfect stitches.)

There is no such thing as perfect.

Even my leaf. It was beautiful, but it was not perfect. There was a knot on the underside.

And even if there wasn't a knot—if I was good enough to cover up that loose thread—would that make it perfect? Not really. Because the loose thread would still be there. You just wouldn't be able to see it.

Maybe everything in life had its messy bits. Things other people didn't see. Or didn't know they didn't know. Or didn't want to think about.

Maybe that was exactly the reason I had to think about them.

On the way home from school the next day, I told Patrick what I'd decided.

He looked shocked at first, and then really, really happy, and then serious. All in about two seconds.

"You sure, Jules?" he said anxiously. "You sure you're okay with that?"

I nodded. I didn't want to talk about it—I might change my mind again.

He said I was a double genius, and our project would be even better because now we'd have tape of the moths emerging. "And you can sew your picture just like you drew it," he said. "You won't have to leave the moth out."

Patrick always said "sew" when he meant "embroider." It bugged me a little, but I guess they must have seemed like the same thing to him. Weird, when he was so hyper about words.

Then he looked more solemn. "I'll do it, Jules," he said. "You can go up to your room, or whatever. You don't have to be there when—when—"

"No," I said. "I want us to do it together."

Something about what Mr. Maxwell had said, and how I felt about the worms—I wanted to be responsible.

"By the way, I've been doing some more thinking," Patrick said, "about—you know, Susan B. Anthony."

We'd never said anything about that e-mail he'd sent me. But I knew that he knew that I knew—well, that I'd appreciated it.

"Pizza," he said.

Pizza? Honestly, just when I thought I had Patrick figured out . . .

He waited for me to say something, and when I didn't, he went on. "Pizza is, like, totally American, right? But it started out Italian. And now everyone thinks of it as American."

"So?" I didn't see what he was getting at.

"Well, between that Susan B. Anthony dress and us doing this project for Wiggle—maybe someday people will think of making your own silk as a really American thing to do."

Oh, brother. Him and his ideas. But I couldn't help smiling. "I kind of doubt it," I said. "Still, you never know."

"Honestly, Jules, I've always thought it was so cool that your family has all this Korean stuff. It makes things much more interesting. Not like my family. We're just plain old nothing American."

I thought about that for a second. "Patrick, that can't be right. Your family must have come from somewhere else, even if it was ages ago. I mean, everyone comes from somewhere else. Even the Native Americans came from Asia, remember?" Part of our social studies unit.

"I guess so," Patrick said doubtfully. He frowned. "I think my grandma's grandma came from Ireland. But there's a bunch of other stuff mixed in — English and French and some German, maybe." He brightened up. "Maybe I'll make it a project — finding out my family tree."

He grinned at me. "Probably be even harder than finding a mulberry tree."

When we got home, Patrick tore a sheet of paper into tiny pieces. He numbered the pieces from one to twenty-six. Meanwhile, I opened up the egg cartons; I had to use scissors to cut the webbing, but it wasn't hard.

Patrick put one number randomly in the

egg-carton pocket with each cocoon. He did this without me looking.

"Okay, Jules," he said. "They're ready."

I was going to pick five numbers. This was how we'd decided to choose the cocoons for boiling. Patrick's idea again.

I stood with my back to the aquarium and said the numbers really fast, without thinking, to make it even more random.

"Twelve, seventeen, four, nine, twenty-three."

"Wait—what were the last two? You were going too fast."

I gritted my teeth. "Nine and twenty-three," I said.

I turned around. Patrick had the five cocoons in his hands.

My mom took out a pot. I filled it with cold water and put it on the stove. Patrick stood next to me and handed me the cocoons one by one. I cupped each cocoon in my hand for a second and wondered, Was this the one with the wider stripes? Or one of the big guys?

I said goodbye to each one—silently, of course —before I put it in the pot. I might not have minded saying goodbye out loud in front of Patrick; he seemed to understand—he was being very quiet and sort of respectful. But my mom was there, too, and I didn't think *she* would have understood. She'd probably have thought I was nuts.

At last it was time.

I was lucky in a way. It wasn't like Mr. Maxwell's chicken. It wouldn't be all bloody and horrible. The water would heat up slowly—it'd be nice and warm for a while, and Patrick had told me (about a million times) that the worms wouldn't feel a thing.

I whispered a final goodbye in my head. Then I put the lid on the pot.

And turned on the burner.

We kept working. I was a little numb, which was a good thing. We rearranged the remaining cocoons so we had one empty egg carton. After the water had boiled for five minutes, we turned the burner down. Then my mom showed us how to stir the cocoons with a stick. As she stirred, the silk started coming apart in sort of a mass. The stick, from a bush in our backyard, was rough and had little twigs on it, and pretty soon she was able to pick up a single strand.

Then Patrick and I each tried, and between the three of us we finally separated out five strands, one from each cocoon.

My mom took over again. She pulled the five strands and twisted them together at the same time. When she had a couple of feet of twisted thread, she handed the end to me. I held a wooden spool and started winding the thread onto it.

It took *forever*. I couldn't believe how *long* the strands were! We pulled and twisted and wound and pulled and twisted and wound, and the silk never seemed to end. I got so tired of it that I even let Kenny do some. I was faster at twisting and winding than either Kenny or Patrick, but my mom was *way* faster than any of us.

Kenny got bored quickly. He stood behind me and made stupid faces while Patrick was taping me — he did it twice, and Patrick had to stop the camcorder each time. I was about to yell at Kenny when I got a better idea.

"Kenny, I'm busy twisting," I said. "Would you count down for Patrick while he films?"

I gave him my watch. He went and stood next to Patrick, and counted down with his fingers like he'd seen me do, and Patrick finally got some decent tape.

After we'd been twisting for almost two hours, I started to feel a little funny. The feeling got stronger until at last I stopped and stood up. "I'm taking a break," I said quietly and looked at Patrick. "You finish up."

"Okay," he answered just as quietly.

He knew what I was thinking. The cocoons had gotten smaller and smaller, and pretty soon we would get to where we'd unreeled enough silk to be able to see the dead pupae. I didn't want to see them. That wasn't very brave, but I'd done the best I could, and the thought of seeing them like that was too much for me.

I went up to my room and sat on the edge of my bed.

They were just worms.

But they were *my* worms.

I'd taken care of them, fed them, worried about

them, watched them grow. And now they'd never get to be moths. I knew I would appreciate the heck out of that silk. But would that be enough to take away the feeling in my stomach—half-numb and half-sick?

Kenny appeared in the doorway. "Julia? Are you sad? Are you going to cry?"

Of course I was sad. "*Leave me alone,*" I said in the coldest voice I could manage.

He hesitated for a moment. "But I got something for you." He held out a closed fist.

"What is it?" Couldn't be much of anything, he was just a baby.

He opened his hand. "Connecticut," he said.

SIXTEEN

KENNY DROPPED the quarter into my hand. It was a little sweaty.

I looked at the tree on the back of the quarter. The branches were as pretty as ever—so tiny. Like strands of silk.

"At first I wasn't going to give it to you," Kenny said. "Because I wanna collect them, too. Just like you and Patrick. But now I want you to have it. Except, will you help me start my own collection?"

It hurt a little when I tried to swallow. I cleared my throat. "Sure, Kenny." I went over to my shelf and took down my money box. "You can get started right away. I've got Illinois here, and New York, too—you can have them."

Kenny beamed as he took the two coins. "Julia, you know Connecticut is my favorite quarter," he said.

"Because of the tree?"

"No, because of the story. I heard Patrick tell it to you. Will you tell it to me again? Please?"

So I did. I told him about how the British didn't want Connecticut to have its own government charter, and about the candles getting blown out, and the charter getting hidden in the hollow of a big tree. The tree on the back of the quarter.

"Cool," Kenny said.

From downstairs I could hear Patrick's voice.

"Yum," he was saying. "Thanks, Mrs. Song."

He had gotten his bite of kimchee.

The moths emerged, white all over except for their black eyes. I was surprised to see how fat their bodies were. I'd seen pictures before, but I guess I thought ours would be different somehow. They weren't slim and graceful like a butterfly; instead, they were squat and chunky. But their feelers were pretty, with delicate featherings almost like lace. I knew just how I'd embroider them, with tiny outline stitches. And they had adorable little teddy bear faces.

Patrick reminded me that the moths wouldn't eat at all. They didn't even fly. All they did was mate and lay eggs, and they lived for only about ten days.

Ten days? It hardly seemed worth the trouble — all the work of spinning a cocoon. But then I figured that ten days for them was like seventy or eighty years for us. A whole lifetime. I guess if I were a moth, I'd think it was worth it.

Seven of the moths were almost twice as big as the rest. Patrick got really excited about that. "The big ones are the females," he said. He reached into the aquarium and gently picked one up. He looked at me a little sheepishly. "No phobia," he said. "I don't mind bugs at all."

For once, I was the one using the camcorder. I videotaped Patrick holding a moth.

* * *

A few days later, the moths mated and started laying eggs.

Hundreds of them. Maybe even thousands. Little gray seeds just like the ones we'd gotten in the mail.

What were we going to do with the eggs? We couldn't keep thousands of caterpillars. If we released them around where we lived, they'd never be able to find any mulberry leaves—they'd just die. Unless we took them to Mr. Dixon's house. And thousands of caterpillars on his little tree—they'd eat it to death.

Mr. Maxwell came to our rescue. He found a place that would take our eggs—a university lab that did research into sericulture. "That's the scientific word for silk farming," Patrick said. We mailed our egg cartons to the lab—the moths had laid the eggs in the pockets—and got a nice thank-you letter back, which Patrick put in our project album.

Besides the letter and the photos, the album held the brochure that had come with the eggs and one other thing: Kenny's pages and pages of temperature recordings. That had been my idea, but I was almost sorry I'd suggested it: Kenny was so proud to have them in the album that he asked to look at it about a million times a day. I had to make sure that his hands were clean and that he always gave it back to me when he was finished.

When the moths died, we dug little holes for them under a bush in front of my house, next to where Patrick had buried the five pupae earlier. He'd done that entirely on his own after the unreeling was finished, and showed me the spot later. I thought it was super-nice of him. He wondered if we should bury the moths under Mr. Dixon's mulberry tree, so their decomposing bodies would help sustain the tree, but we decided it would be a little weird, carrying all those dead moths over to his house. I mean, what would we say? "Mr. Dixon, can we please make a moth cemetery under your tree?"

We put a moth in each hole and gently covered them with dirt. I felt a little sad, but not too bad, because they'd done everything they would have wanted to do. It was probably stupid of me, but I wished that somehow they knew—how, because of those five worms, the rest of them got to live and mate and lay eggs.

They couldn't know, of course.

I'd just have to do the knowing for them.

Our project turned out great. Patrick's videotape wobbled in only a few places. Otherwise, it was really professional-looking. He'd taken the tape into the technology lab at school, and Mrs. Moran, our tech teacher, had helped him edit it.

My mom and I picked a nice blue fabric for the background of my embroidery. The final picture ended up being even fancier than my original sketch, because I decided to show several different stages of the caterpillars.

I did little French knots for the eggs using black floss. Next to the eggs I did tiny outline stitches, also in black, to make a newly hatched caterpillar. Underneath that I used gray thread to make a week-old caterpillar, and underneath *that* I used gray and green and black for a big caterpillar in the stage just before it started to spin.

I kept thinking while I was embroidering how each of the stages had a special meaning for me. The egg—that was like my mom giving us the idea. The smallest caterpillar, barely a little black squiggle, kind of weak and wimpy-looking—that was when I was trying to get out of doing the project. The medium-sized caterpillar was when I'd decided we should go ahead, but I still wasn't crazy about it. And the biggest caterpillar showed how I'd gotten to love them all. Around the caterpillars I embroidered two mulberry leaves, which was my way of giving credit to Mr. Dixon for his help.

My cocoon was the best cocoon ever in the history of embroidery. (I'm only guessing that. But my mom said she'd never seen an embroidered cocoon before, so maybe it was the *first* in history, as well as the best.) I used outline stitches and about a million satin stitches. The silk was a grayish white color. My mom explained that it was called "raw" silk because it hadn't been professionally processed. It wasn't perfectly smooth—it had little wisps and blebs here and there. I liked that; it looked homemade, but in a good way. Like how you know even before you taste them that homemade brownies are going to be better than the packaged kind.

And finally I used cream-colored floss to

embroider a moth, with gray antennae and black eyes.

I thought of the moth as both the end and the beginning—the end of our project but the beginning of a whole new cycle. So if the moth was like the future, would the eggs be the past? Maybe it didn't start with my mom giving us the idea. Maybe it went all the way back to her grandmother, raising silkworms in Korea, which was really where my mom had gotten the idea, right? And where had my great-grandmother gotten the idea? From her mother or grandmother? And how had that person gotten the idea in the first place?

Sheesh. Even when I was trying to keep my thoughts all nice and organized, they started jostling around and making me dizzy. . . .

Boy, did it take me a long time to finish. It was a good thing school had let out in early June—I was embroidering practically every minute for two solid weeks to get the picture finished in time. It seemed like I picked out *way* more stitches than I put in, and once I had to undo almost half of the big caterpillar. I knew in my head what I wanted the final picture to look like, but it was really hard work to get it to turn out that way.

On the back there were some stitches and loops of thread where there shouldn't have been. But I was going to keep practicing. One of these years, I promised myself, I'd enter a project that looked exactly the same on both sides, the way they'd done it in old-time Korea, and I'd display it between two pieces of glass so you could see what I'd done, and the judges would be blown away.

Secretly, though, I *liked* that the underneath of my embroidery was kind of messy. I thought all those knots and loops showed how much work I'd done.

Once it was ironed and put in a frame, my picture looked really nice. Between the embroidery, the video, and the album, we had one whale of a project. We called the whole thing "Project Mulberry: An Experiment in Sericulture." The main title was my idea; the subtitle was Patrick's.

The Wiggle Club voted for Project Mulberry as one of the three from the Plainfield chapter for the state fair. The other two were Abby's pies—she'd finally gotten the crust flaky enough—and Kevin with Gossage the Goose.

Once I found out we were going to the fair, I started caring about winning a prize again. Not as much as before, but still a little. Patrick was *hyper-*excited. He never stopped talking the whole way to Springfield, three hours in the car.

At the fair there was a bit of a mix-up. It turned out there was a new category called Ecotherm Farming, for cold-blooded animals. It was so new that it wasn't in the pamphlets, and even Mr. Maxwell hadn't known about it. So we had to withdraw from Animal Husbandry and enter Ecotherm Farming instead, which had only four other projects, and three of them were about honeybees.

We got second place. First place went to a boy from Carbondale who'd started his own mini-aqua-culture farm, raising trout in a pond. He'd been work-ing on it for three years, so Patrick and I agreed it was right that he won.

I think we sort of helped each other there. When we found out we hadn't gotten first place, we were both disappointed, but neither of us wanted to be a bad sport about it. So I tried to be a better sport than Patrick, and he tried to be a better sport than me, and together we ended up feeling pretty good, because, as Mr. Maxwell said, it was really great to take second place with our first-ever project. He and Patrick were delighted that the judges specifically mentioned our efforts to make our silk farm sustainable. I kept the ribbon at my house—it was a very nice ribbon, red with a huge rosette on top—and Patrick kept the fancy certificate.

In the Domestic Arts/Needlework category, my Life Cycle of the Silkworm embroidery didn't win a ribbon. The projects that did win were amazing. The blue ribbon was won by a girl who'd made a quilt with applique pictures of her family's history, starting with a slave ship from Africa. But the judges were very impressed that I'd used homemade silk thread for my picture, so they gave me a Special Citation for Originality.

I thought it was kind of funny that something my great-grandmother had done years and years ago should be considered original. I guess that was part of what Patrick meant when he said that my family's being Korean-American made things more interesting.

Abby's apple pie took third place in the Junior Pie division, and Kevin and Gossage got an Honorable Mention in Poultry. Mr. Maxwell bought everybody triple-dip waffle ice-cream cones, and we also finished off Abby's pie — the judges had eaten only one slice. Altogether, it was a great day for the Plainfield Wiggle Club.

I still felt a little sad whenever I thought about those five poor worms. When I got *too* sad, I'd look at the embroidered picture — my dad had tacked the ribbon to one corner and hung the frame in the living room. I'd look at the cocoon and silently thank the worms for their silk.

It made me feel a little better.

Patrick already had an idea for our next Wiggle project. He wanted us to grow our own cabbage and make kimchee ourselves. I didn't say yes right away; I wanted to think about it a while. It seemed to me we ought to be able to come up with a project that didn't involve either killing or ferocious smells.

After I carried out a brief campaign, my mom agreed to buy happy eggs from Mr. Maxwell. A dozen a week. It took a longer and slightly more difficult campaign, but Patrick also got *his* mom to buy them. His family needed two dozen. Our victory was achieved when Mr. Maxwell said he'd give us a lower price for buying three dozen every week.

Kenny was always very nice to me when I was helping him with his quarters collection. My mom bought him a folder just like mine and Patrick's, and he wrote his name on it and I helped him keep a record of where and when we found his quarters. I told him the stories about the pictures on the backs of the coins. Or if I couldn't remember them, I'd find them on the Internet and read them to him.

If he was being a brat and I wanted him to stop bothering me, I'd say something like, "If you don't quit it right this minute, I won't help you with Massachusetts," but it seemed to me I was saying things like that less and less often. I guess maybe he was growing up.

My mom let us visit Mr. Dixon sometimes, but she never seemed very thrilled about it. The first time we went, we all watched the video together. Patrick and I had seen it before, of course, but it was fun showing it to Mr. Dixon. He was very impressed, and I have to say I thought it was impressive, too. All those little moments coming together on film—from an almost empty aquarium at the beginning to me holding up my embroidery at the end. Patrick and I couldn't help grinning at each other when the tape finished.

Mr. Dixon got a pound dog—a scraggly-looking friendly little mutt named Cosmo—and Patrick and I dog-sat for him when Mr. Dixon went out of town to visit his grandchildren. One time Mr. Dixon sent us home with some fresh mulberries. They looked like long purple blackberries, and tasted a little like them, too, but with none of those annoying seeds inside. Another time he made mulberry ice cream for us. He was right—it was the best ice cream in the world.

I asked my mom to write down some recipes for

Korean food, and I took them to Mr. Dixon, hoping he would try them out sometime. That way he'd see that Korean food wasn't the same as Chinese food.

I wasn't sure if my mom letting us visit him meant she wasn't a racist after all. I didn't know—but at least I *knew* I didn't know. If she was, maybe she was starting to change, at least a little. She loved the mulberries; she said they reminded her of when she was a girl in Korea. One of these days I wanted to ask her if we could have Mr. Dixon over for dinner, but not for a while yet.

How she felt about Mrs. Roberts and Mr. Dixon and even those soldiers in Korea way back when; how there hadn't been any black people where she'd grown up—all that was the small details. I needed to figure out the big picture, and I wasn't quite sure what it would look like.

But I knew what I *wanted* it to look like—at least partly. And there were things I could do that might help it turn out that way, even if they were only little things.

So I started taking Kenny with us when we went to visit Mr. Dixon.

Not every time.

Just once in a while.

When he wasn't being a snotbrain.

Me: *You forgot to put anything between chapters 15 and 16.*

Ms. Park: *I didn't forget. I did it on purpose. I thought we needed to get things wrapped up toward the end there. Is that okay with you?*

Me: *Yeah. Except I've been thinking—there's tons of stuff that we didn't get a chance to explain. Like some of the names of the characters.*

Ms. Park: *That's easy enough to fix. Here's a list: Mr. Maxwell is named after the principal of my kids' high school; Mrs. Roberts for the base-ball player Roberto Clemente; Mr. Dixon for a neighbor—*

Me: *No, that's not what I meant; I was only using it as an example. What I'm trying to say is that,* *no matter how long we made these sections, we could never explain everything in the story.*

Ms. Park: *Bingo.*

Me: *And if you added it all up, we really only explained a tiny, tiny bit! So why did we even bother trying?*

Ms. Park: *Well, as you said at the very beginning, some readers like to know the inside story, even if it's not the whole thing. But besides that, I think it's good for people to know that there is an inside story, and to decide for themselves when it's important to know.*

Me: *Isn't it always important?*

Ms. Park: *That's a tough one. I think . . . in life, yes. The more you know about things, the more you can appreciate them. But I have to admit that with stories I'm almost never interested in the inside story. If I were the one reading, I'd have* *skipped all these parts—I just want the story itself.*

Me: *Really? You're kidding!*

Ms. Park: *Nope.*

Me: *Sheesh. That seems so weird to me. But I should have expected it from you.*

Ms. Park: *What's that supposed to mean?*

Me: *Never mind. I've got one last question. That part about not knowing whether my mom is racist or not—that bugs me.*

Ms. Park: *I think you're going to keep working on it.*

Me: *How? Is there going to be a sequel?*

Ms. Park: *Well, no, that's not what I had in mind. But your story could continue in the minds* of the readers. They can keep thinking about you and what might happen to you.

Me: *You think they'll do that?*

Ms. Park: *Not all of them. But some of them might.*

Me: *I like that.*

Ms. Park: *Me, too.*

Me: *How many? How many of them will keep thinking about me?*

Ms. Park: *Good grief, I have no idea.*

Me: *Just guess. A wild guess.*

Ms. Park: *There's no way of knowing.*

Me: *Ten? Fifty? A thousand? You don't have any idea?*

Ms. Park: *You're being ridiculous. If we have to continue this discussion, we should do it later, in private.*

Me: *Fine. I'll meet you outside.*

AUTHOR'S NOTE

Below are the books mentioned in the story, listed alphabetically by author. The page numbers in parentheses indicate where in the text the book is mentioned.

Cansdale, C.H.C. *Cocoon Silk: A Manual for Those Employed in the Silk Industry*. London: Sir I. Pitman & Sons, Ltd., 1937. (p. 89)

Enright, Elizabeth. *Then There Were Five*. New York: Puffin Books, 1997. (p. 115)

Hoban, Russell. *The Mouse and His Child*. New York: Arthur A. Levine Books, 2001. (p. 142)

Holt, Kimberly Willis. *When Zachary Beaver Came to Town*. New York: Henry Holt & Company, 1999. (p. 21)

Johnson, Sylvia A. *Silkworms*. Minneapolis: Lerner Publications, 1982. (p. 89)

O'Dell, Scott. *Island of the Blue Dolphins*. Boston: Houghton Mifflin Company, 1990. (p. 85)

The quotations on page 195 are not from Sylvia Johnson's book. They are fictional quotes based on fact.

The model for Mr. Maxwell's farm is Joel Salatin's Polyface Farm in northern Virginia. I first read about Polyface in an article by Michael Pollan in the September 2002 issue of *Gourmet*.

I had a lot of help doing the hands-on research for this story. My parents, Ed and Susie Park, raised one set of silkworms for me; Melanie and Craig Park, my sister-in-law and nephew, raised another. Special thanks to Melanie who, on learning that mulberry leaves were not available, cooked gallons and gallons of artificial silkworm food. I ordered silkworm eggs from the Carolina Biological Supply Company, www.carolina.com. My dad kept a diary of the worms' progress; my mom helped him spin the silk into thread; Craig took photos.

The reason my family raised the silkworms for me is because, as Julia guessed, I do indeed have a worm phobia like Patrick's. After writing this story, I can honestly say that I like them a little better now. But only a little.

Marsha Hayles and Vivian Vande Velde read early versions of this story and offered much in the way of suggestion and encouragement. My writing communities, both online and in person, are a constant source of support. Of great inspiration to me were many discussions about form and structure with other writers and illustrators; special thanks to David Wiesner for design advice and overall genius.

I was fortunate to grow up in a family that believed fiercely in racial equality. However, as both a child and an adult, I witnessed many episodes of racism between Asians and blacks, going both ways. Most disturbing of all to me were the news reports of the violence between the two groups in New York City and Los Angeles in the 1990s. As with any problem, awareness and discussion are the first steps toward healing, and my hope is that this book might be one of those small steps.

Award-winning fiction from
Karen Cushman

Newbery Medal
Winner

Newbery Honor
Book

When life gives you lemons, make lemonade and read all of the books in the Lemonade War series by **Jackie Davies**!

Award-winning stories by **Gary D. Schmidt**
not to be missed!

Newbery Honor
Book

Newbery Honor
Book

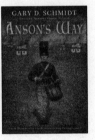